She Built Ships During WW II

Historical Fiction by
Jeane Slone

ESL revision by
Michelle Deya Knoop

SHE BUILT SHIPS DURING WORLD WAR II (ESL Version)
Copyright 2016 ESL Publishing, LLC

ISBN 978-0-9838154-8-8
Library of Congress Control Number: 2016910048

Printed in the United State of America

Cover Design: Jelehla Ziemba/Word Art: JZ@ZWordArt.com

Front Cover: *SS John W. Brown,* Liberty Ship
Back Cover: Black welder: 22-year-old Gladys Thews of Richmond, California, taken by Emmanuel Joseph, Franklin Delano Roosevelt Presidential Library collection; Wendy the Welder, Dorothy Price, Runner-up, "Joan of Arc" welding contest, Richmond Kaiser Shipyard #3, July, 1943. Permission from The Richmond Museum of History, Richmond, CA; Ink drawing of Mine Okubo from her book *Citizen 13660,* 1946, published by University of Washington Press with permission from her estate, Seiko Buckingham.

This novel is historically accurate. All the characters have been fictionalized.

Contents

Acknowledgments

I would like to thank the following people who helped make this historical fiction:

Byung K. (Tony) Chung, a Korean businessman who had a vision and helped produce this book for ESL students.

Michelle Deya Knoop, who put in many hours to make this book possible for students all over the world.

Cris Wanzer, Manuscripts To Go, a creative perfectionist. (ManuscriptsToGo.com)

Sivani Lloyd and Tomeko Yabumoto, ESL teachers

Richmond Museum of History, Richmond, CA

Rosie the Riveter/WW II Home Front National Historical Park, Richmond, CA

Ranger Thaddeus Shay, for his informative tour of Port Chicago, CA

Bancroft Library, UC Berkeley, CA

Rosie the Riveter oral history website: http://vm136.lib.berkeley.edu/BANC/ROHO/projects/rosie/

The tour of the *SS Red Oak* Victory Ship, Richmond, CA and *SS Jeremiah O'Brien* Liberty Ship, San Francisco, CA

The Japanese-American National Museum in Los Angeles, exhibit of the Japanese-American internment

The Japanese-American Legacy oral history project, Tom Ikeda, director: www.densho.org

Benjamin Whitaker, welding teacher at Santa Rosa Junior College, Santa Rosa, CA

Redwood Writers branch of California Writer's Club, Santa Rosa, CA

— Jeane Slone

Acknowledgments

Thanks to Byung K. (Tony) Chung for dreaming up this project and for making it happen.

Enormous appreciation to all of you hardworking students of English.

Many thanks to Jeane Slone for writing this little story down and for entrusting me with its revision.

— Michelle Knoop

Introduction

This dramatic, personal story presents common vocabulary and structure while offering the reader a taste of what life was like during World War II: for women working at home and in the shipyards; Japanese-Americans interned in camps and those who volunteered as soldiers; Black-American pilots, soldiers, and dock loaders; and for the average White American family. It represents both traditional and progressive values of the time, and depicts typical and true scenes of racial and gender discrimination. Finally, the novel movingly portrays how the nation rallied together to win the war against its enemies abroad, in spite of great social and political conflict at home.

Because Americans are grappling with many of these same issues today, the history of how we handled these conflicts in the past can shed light on how we want to engage with our present.

The book offers rich opportunities for discussion and writing. The companion workbook has vocabulary, comprehension, critical thinking, and discussion topics, which coincide with each chapter of the novel.

In addition, the book is arranged in 16 chapters of fairly equal length to make it convenient to teach a chapter a week for a typical semester-length class.

Chapter 1: Home Life

Every night when Joe came home from work, he would ask me how my day had gone and whether the children had done anything bad. I would tell him if our little three-year-old Billy had given me any problems. If he had, Joe would put him over his knee and give him a spanking. Edna, four years old, rarely misbehaved, although she did sometimes get on my nerves.

One evening, I got the children to bed early so I could listen to the radio and knit more wool diapers for Billy. There were never enough. Why, oh why wouldn't he use the toilet like Edna? She had trained nice and young. I wished my sister Diana still lived nearby, so we could talk about my troubles. My friend Sumi's son was already trained. Sumi was such an intelligent, practical person, and I wanted to ask her how she had done it. I certainly couldn't discuss Billy's potty training with Joe. He would just give me a look and say, "That's your problem, woman."

Joe walked in and turned off the radio.

I said softly, "Joe, I was listening to that." I clicked my knitting needles together fast and hard, tightly wrapping the gray yarn. "I think I'll go to Sumi's store tomorrow. The children love seeing her new Scottish terrier dog," I said a little louder.

Joe narrowed his eyes at me, causing his mustache to twitch. "Jeeesus, what kind of name is Sumi?"

"She's Japanese," I mumbled as he went back to his

workshop in the garage. I didn't like it when he swore.

In the morning, Edna rushed into the kitchen with her long, brown pigtails bouncing. "Billy keeps pinching me, Mommy. Make him stop!"

"Pinch him back, and leave me alone; I have to do the dishes." I filled the sink with our breakfast bowls.

"Can we go see Fala?" Billy asked, grabbing my legs.

"Only if you're nice to your sister."

Sumi had a Scottish terrier just like President Roosevelt's dog, and had given it the same name, "Fala." When I told her I thought that was nice, she said, "We have a great president. I wanted to have a dog like his to remind the whole family what a wonderful country this is."

I pushed my curly brown hair behind my ears, put Ivory soap into a dirty pot and ran water into it, then picked up one of the bubbles and blew it into the air, wishing I was inside it, floating away.

Billy skipped toward Edna, yelling, "We get to see Fala and Frankie today!"

The bubble popped and I wiped my hands on my apron. I reached into the cabinet and shook the cardboard oatmeal container. Hearing it was almost empty, I got my pencil from on top of the refrigerator and wrote "oatmeal" on the back of a used, torn envelope. I added a few more items on the list to bring to the Matsumotos' grocery store.

Soon I told Edna, "Put your shoes on and help Billy with his. I'll get the grocery cart."

"I get first ride," Billy said, jumping up and down on an old, handmade braided rug in the hallway.

"You always get to be first," Edna pouted.

60   As they argued, I went to the hall closet for our coats. It wasn't raining yet, although it was a chilly November that year, 1941.

Tired of their fighting, I held the metal handle of the two-wheeled cart and put Billy inside to keep him quiet.
65   Edna whined and gave me her sulky look.

The cool, breezy air of the small town of Richmond, California, made my green eyes shine with energy. The children kept busy playing as we walked. We watched an orange cat walk by, and saw an occasional bird in the
70   leaves of the walnut trees lining the sidewalk. When we reached the Matsumotos' store, I pulled the heavy door open and an old bell rang, announcing our arrival.

Little Frankie ran toward us and the boys chased each other around the store. Fala played too, jumping and
75   barking.

Sumi's eyes lit up when she saw me come in. "Hi, Lolly."

"How's your husband, Hiroshi?" I asked as I took off my old green hat.

80   "He's doing well. Very busy with deliveries," Sumi answered as she feather-dusted the many shelves in the store, turning sideways to make room for her large, pregnant belly. "How's your husband?"

"He works long hours at the trucking company, but I
85   can't complain. I'm glad he has a steady job. I hear unemployment is still very high."

"We should count our blessings," Sumi said, always quick with a positive word.

"Mama, Mama, can I have some candy?" Edna

90   interrupted, pulling at my black polka-dotted skirt.

Sumi reached into one of the many round glass jars of sweets. She pulled out a bright-red lollypop for Edna.

I smiled and thanked Sumi. The boys noticed the gift, and Billy ran to Sumi to ask for candy. Sumi gave him
95   some, then he ran off to the back of the store to share it with Frankie before I could scold him for not saying thank you. I looked at my list and smiled at Sumi as she gathered all the items I read off. Sumi licked her finger, pushing a piece of dark black hair back into her tight bun.

100   "How's your brother's wife in San Pedro?" I asked, remembering that she was also pregnant.

Sumi placed everything into two bags. "She's two and a half weeks past her due date. Hiroshi and I have been praying for her."

105   "It'll be nice for you to have babies almost the same age." I touched Sumi's swollen belly.

Sumi smiled. "Is your sister doing well?"

"She's still not pregnant after three years of trying. I never had that problem," I laughed as my cheeks, always
110   a bit rosy, turned a deep red.

"That's a long time." Sumi got a broom from the corner and swept the already clean floor.

I glanced around the Matsumotos' store. It was cleaner than my house. It was a good thing no one ever came over
115   to see the mess in my living room.

"How did you get Frankie potty trained so early? Edna almost trained herself, but boys are harder to deal with I think."

"The only trick that worked for me was to give him

4

120 candy every time he went in the toilet. I'll give you some of these new candies for Billy." Sumi poured some brightly colored, little round candies from a cardboard tube onto the counter.

"Ooooo, they're pretty." I admired the five different
125 colors of candy circles.

"They're called M&M's. Here, try some." Sumi popped two into my mouth.

"Gosh, chocolate inside!"

"With so many little pieces, you can give Billy one
130 every time he goes in the toilet, then he'll be trained like Frankie." Sumi handed me the tube to keep.

"Thanks. You're so clever. I've spanked him when he goes in his pants, but he keeps doing it anyway. I've got to go finish my ironing and sewing now." I watched as
135 the children ran through the store. "I hope the children take long naps today. I'll try not to snack on these little candies myself. I still haven't lost the 15 pounds I gained in my last pregnancy."

"Thanks for the visit. Try to come more often," Sumi
140 said, and began wiping down the counters.

We walked the 12 long blocks toward home. I pulled on Billy's arm. "Can't you walk faster?"

Edna held tight to the two-wheeled cart. I impatiently picked Billy up and tried to push it while sitting him on
145 my hip. He smiled and kissed my arm, satisfied that he'd gotten his way.

Edna frowned. "Hold me, too."

"Honey, you can drive the cart like a big girl."

Edna liked this grownup game, but she soon got tired.

150   I put Billy down and pushed the cart with both kids hanging on. I started singing to ease our tiredness.

"You are my sunshine, my only sunshine..."

Chapter 2: The Bombing

December, 1941 was rainy and cool. I was looking forward to going to church on Sunday morning, just to get out of the house. The children were in the bath, which gave me time to sew and think. I missed going to the
5 Methodist Church with Mama and Dad. Joe's Catholic Church service was hard to understand because the priest spoke in Latin. I never knew when to kneel or when to stand, and Billy wiggled and pushed at me throughout the entire service. The only good part was that Joe was
10 nice to me when we were in church, and would put his arm around my shoulders and smile.

After the children's bath, I dried Billy off as Edna put a towel around her wet hair. I heard Joe call me.

"Come quick, Lolly! Listen to this news."

15 I left the children and told Edna to help Billy get a shirt on. Joe was in the living room, turning up the radio.

"The first attack began at 7:33 a.m. and several more attacks have followed..."

"What happened, honey?" My voice shook with
20 uncertainty.

"The Japs[1] have bombed Pearl Harbor in Hawaii. Those goddamned yellow snakes!" Joe took a drink of beer from a bottle. "We should send all the Japs back to Japan. They're all spies." The beer dripped down his chin,
25 and he wiped it off with the back of his hand.

---

[1] "Japs" is a negative word for Japanese people.

I went into the kitchen, thinking, *No wonder Joe is drinking so early. This could mean we are entering the war.* But all I really thought about were my good friends Sumi and Frankie, the only Japanese people I knew.

30 "What time is it?" Joe shouted.

I looked at the clock. "It's 9:30, dear." *Why doesn't he look at the clock himself?* I thought.

"Get the children ready, we're going to church." Joe lit a cigarette and smoked it fast and hard.

35

After church, the children and I waited for Joe in the parking lot. The men had grouped together, and stood in a circle talking about the war. I heard Joe say, "Those damn Japs." It made me uncomfortable to hear him talk
40 like that.

At home, I took off my hat and helped the children change into their play clothes, then went into the kitchen to make lunch. Joe sat smoking and listening to the radio news about the bombing.

45 Later, while the children napped, I got a chance to read the paper.

THE FEDERAL BUREAU OF INVESTIGATION LOCATED 737 JAPANESE AND PUT THEM IN FEDERAL CUSTODY. COUCHES WERE CUT AS AGENTS SEARCHED FOR EVIDENCE OF ENEMY
50 SPYING.

I put the paper down. "Oh, no!" escaped from my mouth. "I hope Sumi's family is okay."

"Get me a beer, Lolly," Joe said. "Are you talking

about that Jap store you go to? Tomorrow, buy 50 pounds
of sugar, and not at that Jap store." Joe got up, took a few
dollars from his wallet, then rubbed the new bills together
with his fingers as he gave them to me. "After you get the
sugar, hide it under the bed and don't tell anyone." He
pointed his finger at me. "Stop shopping at that Jap store.
Not one penny of my hard-earned money is going to
those people."

I pressed my lips together to hold in my anger. Who
would I tell? Sumi was the only friend I had, and my
sister lived too far away to talk to. I tried not to cry and
said, "I need to go see how the children are doing in their
room."

"Get me a beer, now!" my husband yelled.

There was so much I wanted to say to Joe, but I knew
he wouldn't listen. It would be nice if Joe's work would
send him far away to do deliveries with his truck. Then I
would only have my children to take care of and could
enjoy some quiet sewing. How could Sumi and Hiroshi's
store be bad? They loved America. They even had a big
American flag out in front of their store. They showed
more patriotism than we did.

The next morning, I looked outside after Joe left for
work, and decided that the clouds floating by did not
show signs of rain. It was breezy out, and the leaves blew
around the street.

"Get your coats, let's go to Sumi's."

"Oh, goody!" Billy lifted his arms and turned in a
circle. "I can play tag with Frankie."

"I'll get more candy!" Edna clapped.

We entered the store under the American flag, and I

85   helped the children pull the heavy door shut.

"Sumi, I've been worried. Have the police come by?" I gripped the edge of the counter.

"No, they haven't, but we're not afraid. We were born here and we're glad the police are getting rid of all the
90   spies. Look at this article in our Japanese-American newspaper," she said, handing me the paper.

THE JAPANESE EMPIRE MUST BE DEFEATED. THE BOMBING OF INNOCENT PEOPLE IN A SURPRISE ATTACK WITHOUT
95   EVEN A HINT OF DECLARING WAR CAN NEVER BE FORGOTTEN. THESE ARE DARK DAYS. THERE IS SUSPICION BECAUSE WE LOOK LIKE THE ENEMY. BUT HAVING JAPANESE BLOOD MEANS NOTHING NOW. WE CONDEMN OUR ANCESTRAL COUNTRY.
100

I smiled with relief. *The Japanese Americans are just as worried about the war as we are,* I thought.

"We want to defend our country as much as you do," Sumi said as I gave her back the article.

105   "I hope others know that. Sumi, I need a lot of sugar."

"We have only 30 pounds left. Strangers have been coming in all day to buy sugar. Everyone's worried about a shortage since the bombing in Hawaii."

"Oh...no wonder Joe wanted me to get so much."

110   Sumi helped me put 15 pounds of sugar in the cart, gave the children each a sweet, and we started toward the door. "Thanks, Sumi. See you later."

"Bye, Lolly, take care."

While pushing the heavy cart full of sugar and both

115 children, I stopped to read a poster on a telephone pole.

Jap Hunting License
Good for the Whole Hunting Season
No Limits on Kill

120

Oh, my God! How can people be so cruel? I thought.

"What?" Edna said, noticing my upset face.

"Nothing, honey. Here's a new song we can learn: 'Pardon me boys, is this the Chattanooga choo-choo...'"
125 Singing always changed my mood.

On the way home, Billy began to get tired. I put him on my shoulder, telling Edna, "Be a big girl and help me push the cart." I sang the song again so she could learn it.

Edna joined in with her little voice. "Track 29, give me
130 a shine!"

The rhythmic melody soothed Billy as he sucked his thumb and fell asleep. His body felt heavy on me like a wet bag of laundry.

After returning home, I considered telling the children
135 not to say anything to Joe about going to the Matsumotos' store. I never knew what he would do.

A few weeks went by. I sat in the living room sewing up a hole in one of Edna's socks. The children were in bed
140 for the night, sleeping in the next room.

Joe rocked fast in his grandfather's old rocking chair. He waved a *Life Magazine* at me. "Read this article, Lolly.

'How to tell a Jap from a Chinese.' Educate yourself, in case we get invaded." Joe got up, threw the magazine on my lap, and pointed at the pictures. "Japanese have flat noses, yellow complexions, heavy beards, red cheeks, and eyes with folds. Look here," he said, poking his finger at a photo of a Chinese officer. "Parchment-yellow complexion, stronger folds on eyes, less beard, and never has red cheeks."

I looked at the photographs. I couldn't tell the difference, but I nodded at Joe and handed him back the magazine. He threw it on the table, then disappeared into the bathroom. He was in there a long time, and when he came out, he had a satisfied look on his face. I stared at his upper lip.

"There, see? I ain't got[2] no more mustache like the slant-eyes wear!" He moved his lip back and forth with satisfaction.

"I'd better check on the children," I said.

Joe said, "It's getting late. Meet me in the bedroom."

I went to the children's room, putting off going to bed with Joe. It had been a few days since we'd made love, and I was not in the mood. I rarely was. Kneeling down between the children's beds, I kissed each child above their little eyebrows. I bowed my head and prayed silently to myself: *Lord, protect my little ones, but please don't give me any more.*

"Lolly, I'm waiting!"

I got up and went to our bedroom.

---

[2] "Ain't got" here means "don't have." "Ain't" is used in some American dialects and is usually thought of as uneducated.

Watercolor by Joe Fitzgerald, age 8, 1944, Maritime Child
Development Center, Richmond, CA. Courtesy Richmond Museum of
History, Richmond, CA

Chapter 3: Executive Order 9066

As soon as Joe left for work the next day, I stopped my chores and sat on the sofa to listen to the news on the radio. I heard nothing but bad news for Sumi and her family. I made a quick breakfast, wrote a short grocery
5   list, and got the children to hurry to Sumi's by teaching them to skip down the street.

"Hello," Sumi greeted us as she reached into one of the glass jars of candy and gave a Tootsie Roll to each child.

10   "How's your family?" I said, worried.

Not looking at me, Sumi said, "Hiroshi had to go to the police station and give them our camera. Then they searched him for weapons." Her eyes got big as she continued. "We don't have any guns, and never needed
15   any in this neighborhood."

"That's true," I nodded, cracking my knuckles.

"My brother's family in San Pedro was ordered to leave their home and fishing boat, with only two days' notice," Sumi said, still not looking at my shocked face
20   and glancing out the window.

I frowned and looked at my shoes, but could find no words of comfort to say.

Back at home, the rain drummed on the roof. Edna cuddled up to me and we looked at her favorite picture
25   book. Billy stretched out on the floor, trying to build houses from an old deck of cards, but they kept falling

down.

Joe came in from work. Without saying hello, he went straight to the radio and turned it on. I was tired of
30   hearing all the bad news.

"President Roosevelt signed Executive Order 9066 today. All German, Japanese, and Italians must evacuate areas of the West Coast..."

"I'm German!" My eyes opened wide.

35   "You're no longer German, and don't forget it. You're married to me. You're Irish now." Joe tapped his fingers on his chair, clinking his wedding band.

While Joe was in the garage and the children were in bed for the night, I sat down to read the newspaper. The
40   headline was, "Executive Order 9066."[3] Though it never named the Japanese, I understood that it meant they would have to evacuate, but I couldn't understand where to or why. I wanted to ask Joe about it. He acted smart, but he made me feel stupid. His answers were either too
45   short or he went too far, yelling and shaking his finger, which made my ears close up. I put the newspaper down and went into the bedroom to write a letter to my sister, Diana.

50   *Dear Sis:*

How are you doing during this troublesome time? The bombing of Pearl Harbor shook me up pretty bad. It's a good thing Joe made me buy a lot of sugar to keep under the bed,

---

[3] Executive Order 9066 was a law made by President Franklin Roosevelt in 1942, which took away the civil rights of over 100,000 Japanese Americans and forced them to live in "camps" in isolated places in the United States.

because I hear it is now being used for gunpowder, torpedo fuel,
55 *and dynamite. Now that the United States has declared war, I*
am always anxious.

I am friendly with a sweet Japanese woman and her three-
year-old son. She owns a store that I have been shopping at for
over two years. Sumi doesn't have a foreign accent because she
60 *was born here. She's a very patriotic person in spite of all the*
news about Japanese Americans on the radio.

In front of her store there is a big American flag on a tall
pole. You almost have to bend down to get through the door.
The Matsumotos are so American they named their son
65 *Franklin, and even got a Scottish terrier like the president's. I'm*
telling you, Sis, this family has Japanese eyes but an American
heart.

Love, your Sis

70 Joe came in from the garage. "Lolly, it's getting late.
What are you doing?"

I put the letter into an envelope, went to the kitchen to
hide it on top of the refrigerator, then reluctantly returned
to our bedroom and got into bed.

75

A few months later, Joe came home from work with a
big smile on his face.

"Can you teach me to play jacks?"Billy asked him,
feeling his father's good mood.

80 Joe laughed. "Sure, sport, you get 'em out and I'll meet
you in your room."

I was confused. Joe usually came home tired and

16

irritable.

"Did you get a raise at work, honey?" I asked.

85 "No, I'm not going back to that trucking job again." He smiled at me.

"Oh, my God. Joe, did you get fired?"

"No, stupid," he said. "I joined the Navy on my lunch hour."

90 "The Navy?" I replied, my eyes wide.

"I'd rather join now than wait for my number to come up."

I turned away from him and looked at the cracks in the floor. "But you have a family. You can't be drafted."

95 "Yes siree, the United States Navy." He tapped his fingertips together.

I chewed on a fingernail to hide the fear in my eyes.

"I'll be shipping out in a few weeks."

Joe went into the kids' room. I heard laughter as they 100 all played together.

A tear ran down my face. I pulled the dishes out and set the table. "Dinnertime..." I called weakly.

Joe came in and saw my watery eyes. "I've got to do my part to beat those Japs and Nazis."

105 That night, I embraced Joe tightly and let my tears flow. He put his big hands on my face. "You know how much I love you, don't you, honey?" he said.

"Yes, but how will I get by alone with Edna and Billy?"

110 "You'll be okay," he said, and kissed me.

One morning a few weeks later, Joe went out to get the newspaper. I looked through the cabinets and found ingredients to make a coffee cake. Joe would be pleased to have warm cake with his paper on his last day home.

115　When he returned, he threw down the *San Francisco Examiner* and said smugly, "Now I don't have to worry about you visiting that Jap family when I'm gone."

I picked up the newspaper and read the headline: "Japs evacuated from areas of West Coast." I threw the
120　paper down again.

After I put the cake in the oven, I watched as Joe handed Edna the forks to put on the table, while Billy sat in the corner rolling his marbles around.

The next morning, Joe put on his new uniform and we
125　all went to the train station together. As we waited for the train, Joe kissed me so long and tenderly that I hardly noticed the children hitting at our legs.

Soon we were watching the train as it moved slowly away, and we kept waving goodbye even after Joe was
130　gone.

The children began to argue. I took their hands and pulled them to the bus stop. As we sat waiting, I felt my heart pounding in my chest.

Billy, who was holding my hand, let go and wiped his
135　hands on his pants. "Eww, Mommy, your hands are all sweaty."

"Sorry, honey," I said, wiping my hands on my jacket. I swallowed hard as I realized that, for the first time in my
140　life, I was completely on my own.

I allowed the children to sleep in my bed with me every night after Joe left, even though I knew he wouldn't like it. Early one morning as they slept, I read a letter from my sister Diana, from New York.

Dear Lolly,

I am trying to understand your feelings about your Japanese friend, but the Japs are really beating the pants off us in this war. They tricked us by planning an attack on Pearl Harbor right in the middle of peace talks. Lately, our troops had big losses in the Pacific. I heard that Japanese-American farmers are lighting fires in the fields and planting their crops in special patterns to help their fighter pilots find targets.[4] Everyone I know says we can't trust the Japanese because they are barbaric by nature. I think we have to put them all in camps until we win this war. Joe has every right to feel the way he does.

Edwin was drafted a few weeks ago. We guessed it was coming since we don't have children. He was going to enlist anyway. After he left last month, I was lonely, so I got a war job. I know how surprised you must be to read this, since I have never worked a day in my life. But now, I'm riveting airplanes! I rivet the fuselage (this is just a fancy word for the main body of the airplane). A rivet is a heavy metal "gun" that shoots a bolt into the holes of the aircraft. This keeps the plane parts together. I work alongside a woman named Jesse Mankiller. She's a Cherokee Indian. I read in the news that 12,000 American Indians left the reservations to get war jobs in the cities. We joke around a lot during break time. We have to wear a bandana to keep our hair back. I tie mine in front to make it look cuter.

---

[4] There was never any evidence to show this really happened.

I wish I could write more, but I'm falling asleep trying to get used to my upside down work schedule (12 a.m.- 6 a.m.).

175   *Love, Diana*

I set the letter aside and got out a few sheets of writing paper.

180   *Dear Sis:*

I can't imagine you working! How do you find time to do your curls? I can't picture you in overalls. I know the Japanese are winning, but still, why should American-born Japanese be punished? I found out from Sumi that "interned" means
185 *putting the Japanese people in military camps. My friend Sumi is well educated and she agrees with the war against Japan. I read in the newspaper that Attorney General Biddle said that evacuating Japanese Americans would be cruel and illegal. The newspaper reported Lieutenant General DeWitt saying, "An*
190 *American citizen is, after all, an American citizen. I think we can weed out the disloyal from the loyal and lock them up if necessary."*

The FBI, Office of Naval Intelligence, and the Federal Communication Commission informed Roosevelt that Japanese
195 *Americans are no security threat, but he signed Executive Order 9066 anyway. I am so worried for my friend Sumi.*

Well, Diana, enough politics for now. I love you dearly, but I don't agree with you or Joe about this issue.

Love, Lolly

200

I folded the letter and looked out the window.

Riveter Harriet Williams, aka Princess Hiahl-tsa,
posing in her traditional dress.

Chapter 4: Only One Suitcase

Later that morning, I opened the window and looked outside. The blue morning sky hinted that spring was on its way. With new energy, I called to the kids. "Wake up, sleepyheads. Let's visit Sumi and Frankie."

5   As we walked there I saw a large sign nailed to a tree that read:

JAPS, DON'T LET THE SUN SHINE ON YOU HERE.

KEEP MOVING!

10

I hid my horror so as not to upset the children. Upon reaching the Matsumotos' store, I saw a white banner with big, handmade letters stretched across the window that read:

15   **WE ARE AMERICAN!**

I blinked several times to stop my tears as I read the sign, knowing that my friends would probably be interned soon. Billy and Edna ducked under the 20 American flag in the doorway and ran into the store.

Billy yelled, "Frankie, Frankie, I have marbles!"

Sumi smiled at me. "Hi. I'm glad you came."

"Yes, me too. How are you?" I tried to be calm.

"We have a curfew now," Sumi said.

25 "A curfew?"

"All Japanese have to stay inside between nine at night and six in the morning, and are not allowed to travel more than five miles from home. Now Hiroshi can't make his deliveries and we have to be extra careful with 30 money."

When Sumi saw the shocked look on my face, she changed the subject. "Would you like some tea?"

"I'd love some," I said, but my mind was filled with worry, wishing I could do something for her.

35 Sumi placed a mahogany tray in the middle of the store with two cups of tea on it. *There must not be much business if Sumi is serving tea right in the middle of the store,* I thought. I searched the shelves, trying to remember if I needed any groceries, but since Joe had left I'd stopped 40 cooking big meals.

"How's your husband?" Sumi asked.

"I haven't gotten a letter from him yet, so I don't really know."

"I'll pray for his safety." Sumi pulled her dress down 45 over her knees and sipped her tea.

"Thanks," I said, thinking her family needed more prayers than mine.

Sumi and I chatted about the weather, my sister, and anything that had no worry in it. After we finished our 50 tea, I said, "I do need a few things."

"But...you didn't bring your cart."

"I forgot it," I lied.

As the children and I prepared to leave, I tucked the grocery bag under my arm. I knew buying these few things wouldn't help Sumi's family much, but it was all I could do.

A few days later there was another letter from Diana, but still not a word from Joe. I read my sister's letter while the children listened to the radio.

Dear Lolly:

I love my job and I love having my own money to spend. Too bad there is so much being rationed right now. I can't even buy a pair of silk stockings. Lately, we have been riveting the B-17 Flying Fortress. It's a huge airplane that can carry 10 men as well as bomb loads. It's equipped with gunner turrets so the crew can fight and fly at the same time. Edwin is training to be a pilot in the Army Air Corps. When I rivet, I think of him and do a very careful job, because I wouldn't want my husband piloting an airplane that wasn't properly put together.

Since President Roosevelt ordered 50,000 warplanes built, this factory is cranking 'em out 24 hours a day! The factory where we build the planes is as big as a town, and the noise is constant and loud. My ears are still ringing when I get home. I have made lots of new friends at work though.

Love, Diana

As I folded the letter, I tried to picture my sister—who usually wore the latest, stylish hat—in a turban and apron with a rivet gun. The thought made me burst out laughing.

I thought my sister was lucky to have such an interesting job and lots of friends. Although I felt freer with Joe gone, I had trouble keeping a routine, and the house was a mess. It was a little too quiet without him. I worried that if Sumi left, I'd have nobody to talk to.

Riveting

The next morning, the children played peacefully as I listened to the radio and looked through my sewing.

The radio blared:

85 *"All Japanese banks in the U.S. are now closed. The U.S. treasury has frozen all bank accounts owned by people of Japanese ancestry, and they can withdraw no more than $100 a month. They must also secure or sell their houses."*

This alarming broadcast made me change my plans. I
90 put away my sewing and called the children.

At Johnny's Drugstore, I saw a sign displayed across the window:

NO JAPS WANTED HERE!

95

The Jenkins' furniture store had a cardboard sign on its door:

JAPS, KEEP MOVING. THIS IS WHITE
100 ## MAN'S NEIGHBORHOOD!

At the Matsumotos' store hung a new sign:

CLOSEOUT SALE

105

Billy and Edna pulled the door open before I could calm myself.

Hearing the bell ring, Sumi came out, looking very

pregnant.

110   "What's going on, Sumi?" I said, looking around the empty store and at the super low price tags on the shelves.

Sumi's lip trembled. "We have just 10 days to pack up and leave."

115   I reached out and grasped her hand. "I'll help you pack."

"I...I don't need help." She fidgeted with the items on the shelf. "Come upstairs and have some tea while I sort through 15 years of our things. I don't know what to do
120   with it all. We are only allowed to bring one suitcase each when we leave."

"Oh, Sumi, you're only allowed one suitcase?" I said, looking around at all the things. "How can you pack your entire life in one bag?"

125   "Like my husband says, we have to leave our possessions behind, but we still have our dignity and memories to bring with us. *Shikate ga nai.*"

"What?" I had never heard Sumi speak Japanese before.

130   "It can't be helped," she translated, holding back her tears. "Hiroshi had to call the junk man, who gave us pennies for all our furniture."

Upstairs piles of clothes, books, and mementos covered the floor. There were balls of yarn, boxes of old
135   letters, family photos, Christmas and birthday cards, but not one piece of furniture in the room.

"Sorry there's nowhere to sit," Sumi said in a whisper. "The junk man took it all."

"I'm so sorry," I said sadly. "Where are...are they...
140   sending you?" I stammered.

"To San Bruno."

"Will you write to me?" I asked, my voice shaky as I
tried to hold back my tears.

"If we're allowed to."

145   Sumi handed me the tea. My teacup rattled as my
hand shook. I was unable to speak. Then I noticed Fala
sniffing at something. "What's that?" I asked Sumi.

She held up a warrior doll that was posed in a fierce,
fighting stance with a miniature bow and arrow. "It's a
150   *Hinamatsuri* doll."

I picked up the remarkably detailed, four-inch figure,
feeling its smooth ceramic head. The body felt soft. "What
a precious doll." I smoothed down the doll's green
embroidered dress.

155   "Thanks. This collection was handed down from my
mother for *Hinamatsuri*." When she saw my questioning
face, she added, "Japanese Girl's Day. Every year on
March 3rd we display these Hina dolls. Here, I'll show
you."

160   Sumi opened a box. Inside was a collection of dolls, all
dressed in colorful outfits.

"The dolls possess the power to contain bad spirits.
Long ago, they used to be set afloat on a boat down a
river to the sea to take the evil spirits with them. Now,
165   *Hinamatsuri* is a time to pray for a young girl's growth
and happiness."

"They're amazing."

"Could you store my collection until I get back?"

Sumi's dark eyes pleaded.

170   "I think so." I hesitated, wondering where I could hide them from Joe when he came back on leave.

"I need another favor of you," Sumi said, taking the doll I held and placing her in the box with the others.

"Anything, Sumi," I said, feeling the heavy guilt of her
175 internment by my race.

"It's Fala." A small tear ran down her cheek. She wiped it away and forced a smile on her face.

"Umm," I answered as I thought about Joe once again.

"You know we can't take him with us."

180   Edna overheard the conversation. "Mommy, we need a dog!"

I looked at Sumi's sad face and reluctantly agreed. "We could use a watch dog with Joe gone, but it would only be temporary."

185   "What is temporary?" Edna asked, hugging Fala so tightly that he yelped.

"Fala belongs to the Matsumotos. They're going away for a little while and need us to take care of him until they come back."

190   "Like a vacation?" Edna asked as she let go of the little dog.

"Sort of," I said.

3/13/42
Photograph by Dorothea Lange, Oakland, California

Chapter 5: A New Job

As the months went by, I got used to living without my husband. Naptime for the children became my favorite two hours of the day because my time was all mine. I looked through my sewing basket. When the pincushion fell out, Fala picked it up.

"Drop it, Fala!"

He obeyed and I scratched him behind his ears. He barked to remind me to feed him, and followed me into the kitchen. A tear fell down my cheek as I grabbed a can of food and turned the can opener. Fala caught a whiff of the food and ran circles around me until I gave it to him. As I watched him eat, I felt heavy-hearted. I sank into a chair. I missed Sumi, my only friend, who had been taken away. Fala licked my hand, as if trying to comfort me, then settled down at my feet.

I sat looking around the quiet house, and the minutes seemed to drag by. I told myself to stop being sad, and hoped for a letter from Sumi. I got up, turned on the radio, and pinned patterns for the dresses I was sewing. There was a national debate on about the possibility of forcing women to work, like a draft. One of the men on the radio said, "The more women working, the sooner we will win this war."

With my long, heavy scissors I cut through the material for my dress. The dog began barking furiously.

"Fala, stop barking!"

I heard a knock on the front door. Glancing around in a panic, I picked up a sock, and quickly put all the dishes in the sink. Who could it be? I opened the door a little and
30 looked out. A lady in a smartly tailored, tan-and-white striped suit with a card on her jacket that read "Victory Visitor" stood smiling at me with shiny red lips.

"Good afternoon. My name is Mrs. Stephens." She adjusted her well-pressed jacket.

35 "Hello. I am Mrs. O'Brien," I said. "Please come in." I uncomfortably pulled on my housedress. "Would you like a cup of coffee?" I glanced at my sewing mess spread out all over the table.

"I'd love a cup. I'm happy to see that you sew."

40 "I enjoy it. I read about Victory Visitors in last month's issue of *Ladies Home Companion*. I'd like to work for the war effort, but I have two small children and my husband's in the Navy." I filled the coffeepot with water, measured the coffee grounds, and turned up the stove
45 flame.

"I saw your blue star in the window. My husband's in the Navy, too," Mrs. Stephens said.

"Where's he stationed?"

"Somewhere in the Pacific." She frowned.

50 "So is mine. Too bad we don't know exactly where." The coffeepot began to whistle. I poured both of us a steaming cup. "Would you like cream and sugar?"

"Cream please. I'd better skip the sugar. I've been trying to do without it since the shortage. You know, Mrs.
55 O'Brien, with most of our men away, our country is having trouble producing all that is needed to win this war," she said with enthusiasm, accepting the cup I

handed her.

"I've heard about the labor shortage, but my mom always told me that the first duty of a mother is to be with her children. My kids are only three and four. I can't go to work."

"There's a retired schoolteacher nearby who will take care of children so mothers can go to work."

"Nearby?" I questioned, my eyes widening.

"Mrs. Crabtree does a great job with the little ones, and with your fine sewing ability you'd make a wonderful welder."

"I don't even know what welding is." I gulped my hot coffee.

"Welding is just like sewing pieces of fabric together, but instead of thread, you put a strip of hot filler, called bead, to join two pieces of sheet metal. Women can become soldiers just like our men—production soldiers. Besides, it would only be for as long as the war lasts, then we can all go back to being housewives." Mrs. Stephens continued, "There are evening classes in welding at Richmond High School. You can practice, get a certificate, and then get a job at the shipyards."

"At night?" I frowned.

"The training program is only a month and Mrs. Crabtree watches children at night. She even gives them dinner and a bath. After class all you'd have to do is put them in their own beds. Just think, you can make $1.20 an hour as a welder!" Her voice went an octave higher.

"That much?" I was barely getting by with the little Joe sent me, and I never knew when it would come.

33

I was glad I had gotten into the welding class at
90 Richmond High, where I myself had gone to high school,
but I had trouble concentrating. My mind drifted,
worrying about how the children were doing at the
babysitter's and what Joe would say about me taking the
class.

95 "It's quite simple to build a ship," Mr. Cunningham,
the instructor, said with a big smile on his face. "You get
your plan, cut out your pattern, and then prefabricate it.
A lot like sewing,"

I noticed that the class was filled mostly with young
100 women and girls.

"Women have a natural ability with their hands," he
continued, his eyes wandering toward me.

I tried to focus on the lecture, and felt uncomfortable
thinking about another man besides my Joe, but Mr.
105 Cunningham's smooth voice was very attractive.

"A skilled welder can make a good seam almost
anywhere. Now class, let's look at some slides on how to
weld."

I was glad when the lights went off and the slides
110 came on, because I couldn't stop staring at the instructor.
He was quite good looking, even though he wore glasses.
His thick glasses probably gave him 4F status[5] but his
short, black, wavy hair, mustache, and his smile made up
for them.

---

[5] 4F Status meant a man could not be in the armed forces because of
physical, mental, or moral reasons.

115   My old high school had been converted almost overnight into a well-equipped welding school. We practiced our new skills on old scrap metal.

One day, Mr. Cunningham announced, "There is now a new school available for those of you ladies needing
120   care for your young children. Our own Henry J. Kaiser, the founder of the shipyards, has helped subsidize the United States Maritime Commission to build the Maritime Child Development Center."

I raised my hand enthusiastically. "Where is it
125   located?"

Mr. Cunningham smiled at me. "Let's see, I have a few pamphlets here. It's right near the shipyards. I'll pass these out."

I felt guilty leaving the children with the lady down
130   the street, but enrolling Edna and Billy in a real school would be a wonderful solution for all of us. How could I sit home and sew dresses, going gray with worry about the war? After all, it was only temporary, until the war ended.

135   On the last night of class, Mr. Cunningham gave out certificates to those who had passed. I was sweating it until I heard my name, "Lauretta O'Brien." As he shook my hand, I flushed with pride.

Returning home on the night city bus, I felt
140   comfortable in my leather work slacks. It was the first pair of pants I had ever owned. Now I just had to pass the ship-adaptability test, and then I could get my first job.

The next morning, I awoke early to prepare. While going through my welding notebook, I found the school
145   pamphlet. I was happy it was so close to the shipyards, but felt anxious after reading that all children had to be

potty trained in order to enroll.

"Hurry! Today's your first day at the child development center," I said to the kids as I hurriedly ironed
150   Billy's pants.

Edna twirled the end of her straight hair, looking up at
me with her big blue eyes. "What's that?"

"It's a school for children." I put the iron on the stove,
then pulled off Billy's dirty night diaper and pinned on a
155   clean one. "Edna, don't mention anything about Billy's
diapers when we get there. I can't have them turning us
away. I have to work. Why are you still in your
nightgown? We have a bus to catch!"

As I put on my new boy-size work shoes, I watched
160   Edna help Billy get dressed. "Thank you, sweetie."

Billy sucked his thumb.

"Don't suck your thumb. People don't like to see big
boys doing that."

Billy walked slowly, whining about going to school.
165   But when I said we were going to take a bus, his bright-
blue eyes lit up and he walked faster.

Chapter 6: The Child Development Center

Through the bus window, I stared anxiously at the newly painted school building as it came into view. It was large, and the nautical windows made the building seem playful and friendly.

5   Edna pointed with excitement. "Look, Mom, it's like a boat!"

When we got off the bus, the children released my hands and ran to the door. After I pulled it open, Billy's eyes got wider and he sucked his thumb while hiding
10   behind my leg. Edna held on to my hand as I walked slowly up to a long, wooden counter.

"Good morning. Welcome to the Maritime Child Development Center," a cheerful young receptionist said.

Edna squeezed my hand so hard I pulled it away from
15   her. Then she grabbed my pant leg.

Billy jumped up and down, yelling, "Up, Mama, up," hitting my other leg.

I felt my face turn red. Then a proper-looking, older lady wearing a plain dress came toward us.

20   "I'm Mrs. Ginzberg, the director," she said.

As I told her my name, she knelt down to the children's faces, ignoring me. She spoke to them in a soft voice. "What a pretty dress you're wearing. What's your name?"

25   Edna mumbled, "Edna," and picked her nose.

"I'm Billy!"

"Tell me, Billy, what is your favorite toy?"

"Marbles and jacks."

Mrs. Ginzberg smiled widely. "Do you have any
30   pets?"

"We have Fala," Edna added brightly. "It's a
borrowed dog."

I covered up that subject by asking, "Will the children
need shots before coming here?"

35   Mrs. Ginzberg rose and proudly said, "We have a
pediatrician on staff. He'll take care of their immunizations."

Mrs. Ginzberg showed us around the school. I glanced
curiously at the round, yellow porthole-like windows, the
40   child-size drinking fountains, and the small chairs. We
went into a classroom, where children's paintings covered
the walls, as well as most of the windows. Billy went up
to an easel, looked into a milk bottle full of paint, grabbed
a paintbrush, and spattered paint all over a sheet of
45   paper.

I took it from him and slapped his hand. "Billy, don't
touch other people's things!"

Mrs. Ginzberg scolded me. "Mrs. O'Brien, we do not
allow hitting here."

50   I felt my face flush as I looked down at the wooden
floor.

Mrs. Ginzberg took the children's hands and headed
for another classroom, saying to me over her shoulder,
"Mrs. O'Brien, there are some forms for you to fill out at
55   the front desk."

As I filled out papers, I thought about Mrs. Ginzberg's reaction when I had slapped Billy's hand. The idea of not slapping children was ridiculous. It made me wonder about the place, and how they would keep the children in line. Why, I had seen Mrs. Crabtree, the babysitter, spank a child who was misbehaving when I picked up the kids once. Everyone knew it was sometimes necessary.

I took my completed forms and went searching for Mrs. Ginzberg and the children. I found them in a classroom with other children the same age as Edna and Billy. I noticed shelf after shelf of children's books. The children sat in a circle on a large rug. The teacher was reading to them with an expressive voice, and pausing to show the kids the pictures. Edna and Billy were wide-eyed and quiet as they listened to her. I had to admit, all the children seemed to be very well behaved.

Mrs. Ginzberg walked up to me and said, "Your children will be very happy here. This is one of the newest centers. All our teachers are graduates of UC Berkeley, which provides the most current methods in education. Your children will learn many subjects here, including manners and social skills. Tomorrow, come a half hour early so the children can get their immunizations."

"I'm glad to hear that. I'd better go now. I have a test to take at the shipyard," I said, and glanced at an anchor-shaped clock. I looked longingly back at Billy and Edna. There were rows and rows of brand new toys. Maybe the children there were well behaved because there was so much to do.

Before I left, I gave the receptionist a bag for Billy. I said it was clothes, but it was really diapers.

Saying goodbye at the child care center

At the hiring hall, there must have been over 1,200 people wandering around. I had never heard so many different languages or seen so many different races of people before.

I found a sign that read "Shipyard Adaptability Test Station #1" and got into a long line. A half hour passed before I finally reached the front of the line.

A fat man smoking a big cigar said to me, "Here lady, take this 25-pound bucket of scrap metal and carry it around the room."

I picked up the bucket and lugged it around the room, trying to appear as though it wasn't heavy at all. With sweat beading my brow and running down the back of my neck, I returned to the man and tried to hand it to him. He narrowed his eyes, bit hard on his cigar, pointed to the floor, put a check mark on my test card, and yelled, "Next!"

"Where do I go now?" I whispered, out of breath.

He stuck his thumb out to the right.

I got into another line and watched the gal in front of me climb up and down a long ladder against the wall. On my turn, a man timed me with a stopwatch. I was breathing hard as the man handed back my card. I noticed him looking at my heaving chest. I grabbed my card and rushed away, deciding not to ask him where the next station was.

When I looked at my card, I saw that I had passed the adaptability test. Now I had to wait in another line to get my identification badge. While there, I heard two old men speaking loudly.

"Women ain't got no muscle. They can't work hard,

120 and they make the men around them useless," said one of them.

His buddy agreed.

125 I frowned at their stupidity. When my turn came, the photographer took my picture so fast I never got a chance to smile. My badge had all my personal information on it, including my fingerprints. Finally, I stopped at the last station, War Bonds. A young boy asked me a lot of financial questions, then suggested how much I should spend on bonds.

Watercolor by Donald, age 10, 1944, "Outfitting Dock, Richmond Kaiser Shipyard." Courtesy Richmond Museum of History, CA

130 Afterwards, exhausted but happy, I walked the long blocks to the Maritime Child Development Center to pick up the children. I watched Edna sweeping imaginary dirt with a child-size broom into a dustpan held by another little girl. There were many children, yet no fighting like I 135 had seen at Mrs. Crabtree's.

Edna saw me and bounced over to where I stood. "I made lots of friends. Can we come back?" she asked.

"We sure will." I hugged her. "Let's get your brother."

Edna waved at her friend. "See you tomorrow," she 140 called out.

In Billy's classroom, we watched him pushing a truck through small, wooden blocks. He growled at us, "Go away."

Glancing around me, I lowered my voice. "Don't talk 145 to me that way or you're gonna get it. Where's your coat? We've got a bus to catch."

Billy drove his dump truck farther away from us. "I'm sleeping here, like Peter."

Before I could discipline him, Mrs. Ginzberg came into 150 the room. "Hello, Mrs. O'Brien, how was your day?"

"Fine, thanks," I said, trying to cool my temper.

"I'd like a word with you before you leave."

"Has Billy been bad?" I quickly asked.

"No, he's behaving as well as three-year-olds do. His 155 toileting is what I need to discuss with you."

I pressed my lips together, looking down.

"Mrs. O'Brien, Billy is a smart boy, but we both need to get him toilet trained."

My face turned red as she continued.

160 "I want you to go to the store, and buy two playsuits with drop seats and big buttons. That way Billy can undo them himself."

I glanced at the clock. "We must go catch the bus." I tried to hold Billy's hand, but he ran away from me.

165 Mrs. Ginzberg went up to him, knelt down, and said, "Billy, would you like to borrow a small truck, just for the night, to play with at home?"

His eyes brightened as she placed the toy into his hands. I led him easily toward the door, and said,
170 "Thanks, Mrs. Ginzberg."

"You're welcome. Remember, big buttons. Don't forget to get your dinner to bring home. It's meatloaf and baked potatoes today." She walked confidently off to her office.

175 As we waited in the long dinner line, I was grateful that I didn't have to go home and cook, but the children were noisy and restless. I certainly didn't have time to get new pants for Billy. Mrs. Ginzberg had no idea what it was like to be a working mother.

Chapter 7: A Horse Stable

The next morning, after dropping off the children at the center, I walked to the shipyard and stood in a long line to get in, wearing my badge on my jacket. I felt proud that I had passed all the tests. My jacket was the smallest
5 men's size I could find, but it hung loosely all over me. I noticed there were mostly women in line. I thought that the few men there must have been 4F status. Some walked with limps, others wore glasses. They seemed to be quite an unsightly crew.

10 There were four large Kaiser Richmond shipyards. I was assigned to yard one. I was also assigned a break room locker and a hardhat. I made my way through the crowds of workers and got to the *SS Red Oak* Victory Ship. I followed some people up a narrow ladder. On the first
15 deck, I watched as construction began on the new ship below. The huge metal keel was swarming with hardhats, like ants on a candy wrapper. Above me were seven levels of crisscrossed wooden framework. The hull was held in place by support stocks as it was built.

20 A mean-looking foreman looked at me and growled, "Put on yer hardhat, lady. Follow me."

I held my hands tightly at my sides as we walked past workers and equipment. When we stopped, he handed me a welder's helmet and said, "This is where you'll
25 start."

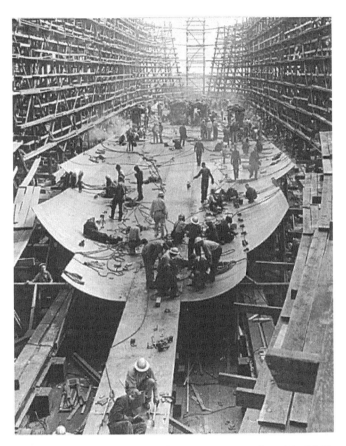

Building the hull at Marinship, CA, September 19, 1942

After he left, I put on the helmet and stood watching the person in front of me weld. I wondered if it was a man or a woman. Then the welder stood up, pushed up the
30   hood to examine the work, and stepped back, bumping into me.

"Excuse me, ma'am," a young girl with a smooth, brown face exclaimed.

"That's okay," I shouted over the hammering and hiss
35   of equipment. "Sorry I got in your way. Hey, aren't you the gal who was in my welding class?"

"Why, sure thing! My name's Hattie." She smiled, revealing her white teeth.

"I'm Lolly. I'm glad I'll be working with another gal
40   instead of some bossy man."

"I know watcha[6] mean!" She put her hood down to finish her beading strip.

Time flew by when we worked together as a team. The noon whistle sounded and we headed to a break room.
45   Hattie went to her locker and got out her lunch bag. I went to mine, took off my gloves and hood, and said, "I've got to find the canteen. I forgot my lunch."

As I made my way across the busy shipyard, cranes circled over my head, and people walked around every
50   which way as truck horns blared. I walked by a group of men.

One whistled and shouted, "Hey, babe, watcha doin' tonight?"

Another added, "Hey, sugar, are you rationed?"

55   I turned red and wondered what in the world made

---

[6] "watcha" is informal speech for "what are you" or "what do you"

me attractive in my welding clothes. I ignored them and got into the canteen line, hoping they would stop.

60 For lunch I bought the "Riveter's Special" for 40 cents, which included two sandwiches, salad, an apple, a pastry, and a cup of hot soup. An oriental man waited on me. There was a handmade label on his jacket that read: I AM CHINESE. He handed me my lunch, and a Chinese lady took my money.

65 Seeing the canteen workers reminded me that I had a letter from Sumi in my pocket. I had been too tired to read it last night after standing in lines at the store trying to find a box of laundry soap. Rationing made shopping difficult. Even when I had a coupon, sometimes there was nothing left to buy.

70 I unfolded Sumi's letter and sipped the warm soup.

To my dear friend Lolly:

I'm sorry I haven't written sooner. I had to find the strength of a "good mood" in order to send you this letter.

75 *A bus brought us to the Tanforan racetrack just outside the city. There is hardly room for the three of us in this small stable. The smell of horse manure is so strong that the first few days here I threw up a lot. I guess pregnancy and bad smells don't go well together. Hiroshi used an old apple crate to make a bench* 80 *for me to sit on outside our door. Now I can get some fresh air, though there's not much sun because our place is located on the north side. I miss the walnut trees on the street outside our store. Now my view is a twisted barbed wire fence with sharp, mean points. Instead of birds in the sky, I see armed guards in* 85 *towers pointing guns at our "homes." We are imprisoned for the crime of having different eyes. After all, I am as American as you are. Lolly, I want to believe in America, but I am feeling*

49

desperately hopeless here. How can I raise children in a horse stable? I am so worried about the baby.

90   *I worry about our store too. Do you know if the Soleskys are watching it for us? Also, I worry about my precious paintings that I left on the wall in my living room. I would worry about Fala, too, but I know you are taking good care of him.*

     Although we left most of our things behind, we still have
95 *our memories. I think about you, your little girl, and how our two boys played together. Frankie talks about Billy every day, even though he has friends to play with here.*

     Please write back soon to cheer me up!

     Your friend, Sumi

100

     I closed my eyes a moment, overwhelmed by the thought of my friend in such a place. It wasn't that long ago that we'd had tea together.

     I wanted to do something to help them, but I couldn't
105 think of what. The idea of Sumi giving birth in a horse stable was very disturbing. When I had read that the Japanese were interned in camps, I had pictured a nice, summer camp kind of place, not a smelly, cramped stable. I felt guilty as I folded up the letter and put it away. I was
110 glad the lunch hour was over so I could go back to work and not think about it anymore. I was just about to stand up when a man sat down next to me.

     "Hi, Lolly. I see you got a job, though I'm not surprised; you were one of the best welders in my class,"
115 Mr. Cunningham said with a flirtatious wink.

     "Hi, Mr. Cunningham. I'm welding on the *SS Red Oak*. Wha-what are you doing at the shipyard?" I stammered, feeling the intensity of his eyes on me.

"I teach safety classes here," he said, giving me a big
120   smile.

The whistle blew and I grabbed my lunch. "I'd better
go. Bye, Mr. Cunningham."

He raised his eyebrows. "Call me Phil."

I smiled and walked away, thinking that he looked
125   like a movie star. It made me feel good that such a man
would flirt with me.

After work I took the bus to the National Dollar Store
to get the pants for Billy so Mrs. Ginzberg would be
satisfied, then went to the center to pick up the children.

130   I said hello to the receptionist and glanced about,
relieved that Mrs. Ginzberg was not around. I placed the
pants in a bag in Billy's small wooden square they called a
"cubbyhole," then got in line at the kitchen to get my
dinner box to bring home before getting the children. Mrs.
135   Ginzberg had told me to do it that way so the kids
wouldn't have to wait in line and become restless.

Back at home that night, I washed the dishes, hung a
load of laundry in the backyard, and got the children to
bed. Exhausted, I collapsed on the sofa to read a letter
140   from Joe that had finally arrived.

Dear Lolly:

*I'm on the ship but can't tell you exactly where we are. I
hope you are managing with the money I sent you. The $99 a*
145   *month is not nearly as much as when I was working for the
trucking company. I hope you'll do okay. I heard all the Japs are
gone and feel a lot better about leaving you now. I'm getting
tired of the food on the ship and I especially miss your delicious
chicken dinners. I've been at sea for many days, watching the*

150   *sun set and rise, rise and set, with no land in sight.*

    I sure miss you and the kids.

    Your loving husband, Joe

    P.S. Why aren't you writing every day?

155   I felt sad about Joe's anger toward Japanese Americans. If only he could see with Sumi's eyes, he wouldn't feel that way. I decided not to think about what he would say about my Negro friend, Hattie. *Not all the good people in this world are Irish*, I thought.

160   Reading the letter again, I could feel Joe's love. *I must try to stay awake tomorrow night so I can write back to him and tell him about my new job*, I decided.

Chapter 8: Flash Burn

It was jumping in the break room during lunch hour the next day. A few of the gals lined up with their arms around each other and sang a new song called "Rosie the Riveter." Hattie and I joined in, while the rest of the gals made a riveting noise with their tongues, singing, "BRRRR" while tapping pencils on the benches. Everyone sang out the chorus together. We sure had a good time. It was more fun working than being stuck at home all day.

After we sang, Hattie and I sat down and ate our sandwiches.

"Do you live in Richmond?" I asked her.

"Yes ma'am. I'm a boarder so I share a room with a married couple. We work opposite shifts, so we take turns in the beds, which stay nice and warm."

"What about the weekends?"

"Saturday I sleep at Keva Theater where my pal Polly sleeps. That way I give the married couple some alone time, if ya'll know what I mean." She winked, then added, "Sundays I sleep on the floor."

I gasped, trying to picture this. "Your friend sleeps in a movie house?"

"Yes ma'am, she's been waiting for a room to rent for almost a month now, but it's cheaper to sleep in the theater 'cause it's only 25 cents to get in. Why, it even costs $1.50 a night for a seat at the barber shop."

"I guess I don't know how good I have it."

"There are about 19 theaters in town, and believe me, there's a lot of cheap sleepin' goin' on. Polly knows which ones are flea houses and which ones ain't. Why, most of the Indians working here sleep over on the other side of the tracks in box cars."

I packed up my lunch and shook my head at Hattie's stories as I walked out of the break room.

After work, I walked to the child development center. Inside I saw two policemen speaking to the director, holding the hand of a dirty-faced little girl about Edna's age.

"We have room for her to sleep upstairs, but I sure hope you find her mother. We are not an orphanage, you know," Mrs. Ginzberg said, shaking a finger at the officers.

"That's our next job, to find the parent. There are children wandering around alone all over the place. And almost every day we find children sleeping in automobiles. Often they're so sleepy we think they've been given some kind of pill to keep them asleep until their mothers get off work."

"Try to tell everyone you know there's a daycare center now, and an automobile is nowhere to leave a young child," Mrs. Ginzberg said disapprovingly.

"We're meeting with the head of the shipyard today for that reason," said the policeman. "Goodnight, ma'am."

The policemen left.

"Come here, darling. Let's get you into a proper bed," Mrs. Ginzberg said to the little girl. "Mrs. O'Brien, please meet me in my office. I need to take this child upstairs."

I wondered uncomfortably whether she had gotten Billy's extra pants. As I sat in Mrs. Ginzberg's office, I
60 read all her diplomas on the wall.

"Hello, Mrs. O'Brien. How are you this evening?" Mrs. Ginzberg said with her formal voice as she entered the office. She sat down at her desk. "Billy keeps wetting himself...he missed going outside today because he had to
65 wait for his pants to dry. He's an intelligent boy, but if we're going to make any progress with his toilet training, you must help. On the weekend you need to take him to the toilet every hour."

"I'll try harder," I said.

70 "Good." She began going through the pile of mail on her desk.

I rose and went out the door, feeling rejected. I had to force myself to say thank you.

The bus ride home was longer than usual. The
75 children were talkative, but I was too exhausted to listen. I was worried about potty training Billy. I should have listened to Sumi and tried the M&M method instead of eating them all myself. While Billy sat on my lap, Edna chatted on about her day. When I felt my lap turn wet, I
80 knew I had a big job ahead of me.

Hattie and I worked well together when there was a piece of sheet metal that needed joining. She welded one side while I welded the other; that way it didn't buckle.
85 The piece we had to do next was about 45 feet long. After I found the right rod, I nodded my hood down and put the rod into the electric stinger. I made a beautiful line of liquid flux beadwork, bringing back a memory of my

mother embroidering the edging of a tablecloth. I made a
90   pass with the rod, then a second. The stinger produced
flying fireworks of cobalt and sparkling gold. The sizzling
noise reminded me of a thick, juicy steak frying on the
stove.

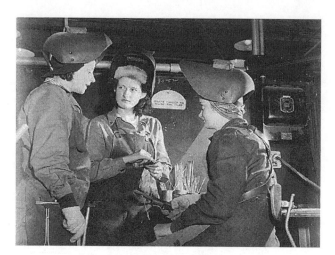

Women welders

Hattie finished her line just as I finished mine. I
95   flipped my hood up as we each chipped the slag with a
hammer, then brushed everything smooth with a wire
brush. We went on to the next piece. I put in a different
size rod this time, nodded my hood down, and again
watched the liquid turn into tiny beads. With the welded
100 line finished, I jerked my neck up to move my welding
hood so I could wipe the sweat off my nose. Suddenly, a
streak of glowing blue light hit the sides of my eyes. A
quick flash had come from Hattie's stinger. I couldn't see.
Panicked, I pulled my hood down and stepped back until
105 I felt the wall. I slid down and sat on the floor to wait for
my vision to come back. After a few minutes, I felt better

and continued welding.

Toward the end of the day, I knew I hadn't escaped the flash burn from Hattie's stinger. As I was getting my lunch box, I felt a sudden, sharp pain in my eyes and groaned.

"What's wrong, honey child?" Hattie rushed over to me.

Breathing hard, I said, "My eyeballs feel like razor blades are slicing them."

Hattie guided me to a bench. "Here, set yourself down. I'll get the foreman." She ran out of the room.

It felt like hours as I sat grinding my teeth in pain. I heard a crack and screamed, "Oh my God, I broke a tooth!"

Then I heard the foreman yelling at me. "Stop grindin' yer teeth! Close yer eyes an' hold on to my arm. I'll drive you to Kaiser Hospital. If you weren't a dame, I'd tell you to lie down, put a sliced potato on 'em, and just ride it out."

My eyes stung worse when I shut them.

I heard Hattie say, "I'll come."

The foreman grunted, "Nigger,[7] I don't need you!"

---

[7] "Nigger" is a strongly negative word for Black or African American people.

Welders

I moaned as he grabbed my arm and dragged me up the metal stairs. Soon I felt the cool air on my face and
130 knew we were on the top deck.

"Would you move faster?" he growled. Then he pushed me into a jeep and we drove off, the pain in my eyes still terrible.

On the ride to the hospital, the foreman said, "Lady, I
135 got some free advice for you. That zigaboo you're friends with is just an animal. Back where I come from we'd string a nigger up[8] every now and then just to keep the

---

[8] "string a nigger up" means to hang a Black person from a tree and kill them, which is called lynching. Lynching happened most frequently in the Southern United States between 1882-1968.

rest of 'em in order. Stay away from them and stick to your own kind."

140   I shivered in the seat, but kept quiet.

Once at the hospital, I rested on a cot with a wet cloth on my eyes. The pills the nurse gave me helped reduce the pain a bit. I began to worry about Billy and Edna. "Nurse, nurse, I need to get my children at the center!" I
145   yelled out into the darkness.

"You are aren't going anywhere, dear."

"But, my children..."

"Where are they?"

"At the Maritime Child Development Center," I said,
150   trying not to rub my eyes.

"I'll telephone over there and see what they can do. Now leave your eyes alone until the medication kicks in and puts you to sleep."

"Billy, Edna..." I moaned, drifting off through the
155   throbbing pain.

The following week, in our first safety class, I watched Mr. Cunningham closely. He was real good looking. He was talking about injuries. He told us, "So far, our Kaiser
160   Hospital treats around 500 work injuries a day, such as eye injuries, bruises, and broken bones. By the way, class, don't forget to take your salt tablets. You will find them at every drinking fountain on the ship. The salt replaces what is lost in your body through perspiration on the job.
165   Over 20 employees have died at work from dehydration. Now I'd like to discuss flash burns and how to prevent

them. You already know you should keep your hoods
down so you won't get flash burns when you're welding,
but it's also important to keep your hood down around
170 other welders, as well."

"What's flash burn like?" Rosa asked.

Mr. Cunningham looked at me. "Mrs. O'Brien, would
you mind telling us about your experience with flash
burns? The class could learn from hearing about the
175 recent accident you had."

I blushed, and described to the class how I got flash
burn, and how it felt.

"Thanks for that excellent description, Mrs. O'Brien.
It's similar to getting a sunburn. You don't feel it until
180 later on. Remember everyone, keep your collars buttoned
up too, so you don't expose your skin. Also, put your
gloves on tight; that way the sparks can't fly down the
cuffs," Mr. Cunningham said.

He was such an intelligent, kind man, I thought,
185 compared to the nasty foreman who had taken me to the
hospital.

He continued his lecture. "The safety commission has
decided that women should not wear jewelry at work,
including wedding rings."

190 The gals groaned when they heard that.

Chapter 9: Flirtation and Flyers

For lunch breaks, I usually allowed myself the luxury of going to the canteen once a week. When I invited Hattie, she said she had to send all her extra money home to her mama. I felt a little guilty, but told myself I had earned it. I loved the sound of loose coins in my pocket. Earning my own paycheck was very satisfying.

While reading the lunch sign, I saw Mr. Cunningham out of the corner of my eye. I quickly ordered, and with food in hand, I headed to the other end of the canteen, as far away from him as I could get.

I heard him call out my name. "Hey, Lolly, sit here."

My heart jumped. The only free spot was right next to him. I hesitated as he moved over and patted the bench.

"How are you doing?" he said, looking into my eyes.

"Fine, Mr. Cunningham," I said, fidgeting with my wedding ring and looking at his clean, well-pressed work shirt. He was a much smaller man than my Joe, but his open face warmed me.

"You've known me long enough now to call me Phil," he said, and offered me his apple.

"No thanks, uh, Phil." I shoved in a bite of my salami sandwich and glanced over at his left hand, noticing that he didn't have a wedding band.

"Did you hear about MacArthur's return? Over 600 ships have been sent to the Philippines to wipe out the rest of the Japanese," he said, waving his arms around energetically.

I smiled slightly. I didn't want to talk about the war. It reminded me of my Joe, and I didn't want to be a widow with two small children.

Phil changed the subject. "There's a good movie playing at the Keva Theater. I'd love to take you there."

"I couldn't. I've got to pick up my kids at the daycare center every night."

"Do they have night care there?"

"They did stay over one night when I had my accident."

"Why don't you tell the daycare you have to work overtime, and see a show with me?" Phil persisted.

"Well, um, you know, umm, Mr., uh, I mean Phil...I am married," I stammered.

"I assumed that, Lolly, but I'm not. I also guess your husband's in the service. It's just a movie. There's nothing wrong with going out with a friend." He lowered his glasses and smiled at me.

"I suppose. I haven't been to a picture show in a very long time."

"Great," he said. "I'll meet you right here on Tuesday, after work."

He took off before I could change my mind.

When the noon whistle blew at work the next day, I climbed up the stairs to the break room. Hattie got out her lunch as I poured my soup into my thermos cup.

55   "Where are you from, Hattie?"

"I'm from Alabama, ma'am."

"You know, you don't have to call me ma'am. It makes me feel uncomfortable. We're about the same age."

"Yes, Lolly, I'm sure glad not to be in Alabama where
60   I have to call White people Miss or Missus. I came here on the Southern Pacific rail with my brother after my husband joined the U.S. Army. At the beginning of my trip all the Coloreds[9] sat behind a black curtain on a long bench. When we switched trains in the West, we were
65   shocked to see a Colored sitting right next to a White![9]

"Back in Alabama, a friend of mine, a Colored nurse, went in front of the Whites to get on the bus, and she was beaten and jailed!" Hattie shook her head sadly as she ate her sandwich. "I got tired of cooking, washing, and
70   ironing for Mrs. Jenkins. Why, I hardly earned enough money to rub two nickels together. I feel free as a dog without a leash living here. But I do miss Alabama in the springtime. You wouldn't believe the flowers every-where."

75   "My husband's on a ship in the Pacific. Where's yours?" I asked.

"My husband's a pilot at the Tuskegee air base in Alabama. My brother's in the Navy. He's stationed right here across the bay at Port Chicago."

80   "I wish my Joe was that close," I said.

---

[9] "Colored" meant Black or African American and "White" meant Caucasian people. In Southern states before the 1960s, Black people were only allowed to sit at the back of public buses and trains, and were not allowed to sit next to White people.

63

"I still can't get over it," Hattie said. "Me sitting here at the same table talking to you. Lord have mercy, this would never have happened in the South." Hattie shook her head, and re-knotted her kerchief in the front as her big, gold hoop earrings jingled.

When our shift was almost over, Hattie got out a letter from her locker. "Can you help me...um...read this? My sweetie is a educated man, but I only made it to the second grade. I had to go to work to help Mama support my eight brothers and sisters after Daddy died."

"Sure, I'd be happy to." I read the letter out loud:

To my Sweetie Pie:

I miss you and dream about you every night. My Negro buddies and I have been working extra hard here at the air base. We know we are being tested and we are competing against the Whites to prove our value, even though most of us are college educated and highly qualified. We are trying to prove to them that our brains are not smaller than theirs and that we are just as good as they are at flying planes. In the other branches of the service, our people end up serving as janitors or work in kitchens and don't get to fight for our country.

My buddies and I talk about how we are fighting a double war; we have to fight for our race as well as our country. I'm ready to serve my country, but why should we be segregated? Why can't we fight together in a mixed regiment and end racial discrimination?

Yancey Williams is in my squadron, and he is quite famous here. He filed a lawsuit to force the U.S. government to let him join the Army Air Corps. Thanks to him, the day after his court appearance, Negro pilots were accepted in the service.

On the trip here, my buddies told me they all sat together,

115 *even though it was not a segregated train. At one of the stops, a White lieutenant ordered them to stand and give their seats to White Italian prisoners of war. Are they better than us? They even built new training facilities here so the Whites wouldn't have to share the runways with us.*

120 *I have only one week left of this grueling five-week flight training to earn my silver wings. I hope you got a job and your brother is watching after you for me. Please try to write to me. I miss you so much!*

Love, your Granger

I gave Hattie the letter. "He sure does love you."

125 Hattie's eyes lit up. "Yes ma'am, I love him too, with all my heart and soul."

"I have an extra V-mail that you could write him back on. By the way, in case you don't know what V-mail is, it is a letter photographed onto microfilm. They say one reel
130 can hold 18,000 letters and saves shipping space for war equipment."

"Why, thank you kindly, I'll let you know if I need it."

Hattie fiddled with the hood on her welding helmet, which sat on the bench next to her. I asked her if her
135 husband knew that she couldn't write. She looked down.

"I'll write it for you," I said.

She burst out, "Why, bless your heart. I can't thank you enough!"

"It's nothing. Can I ask you a question? How did you
140 pass the written part on the welding test?"

"Can you keep a secret?"

"Of course."

65

"Mr. Cunningham asked me the questions after class one day."

145   "You sure seem smart enough to learn to read and write," I said.

"I'll learn someday, maybe when this war's over and I settle down with my sweetie."

Tuskegee Airman

150 At the end of the day I went to the bathroom and slipped on my strawberry-colored dress with the flared skirt. I put on eye makeup and it smeared in the corner of my eye. Rubbing it off turned my eyeball red. I pushed my makeup kit into my purse, wondering what in the world I was doing.

155 I met Phil at the canteen. He was wearing a two-button suit with a vest and Oxford shoes. He looked very handsome. We walked across the street and got into his Ford Model A.[10]

160 "I haven't been in a car since my daddy died two years ago." I spoke nervously as I sat in the clean, polished automobile.

"How's it going for you at work?" he asked as we settled in.

165 "I enjoy the gals. Most of the men are rude though. I don't like the way they look at me, as if I don't have a right to be there because I'm a woman."

"I'm sorry, Lolly. They are not the most educated bunch. I've seen guys smashing light bulbs with rocks, lighting their cigarettes with torches, burning their names 170 into metal, and throwing their leftover lunches overboard. I've even caught guys going over the fence to nearby bars for drinks during work hours. But mostly they're hard-working guys."

175 I told him about my friend Sumi, and that her family was living in a horse stable now at Tanforan. I was curious how he felt about Japanese Americans. It turned out he had a Japanese-American friend named Tom.

---

[10] The Ford Model A was the second car, made and sold by Ford Motors, that many people could afford to buy (the Model T was the first).

"His real name is Toyo. He's Japanese American, Nisei, born here. I used to weld with him before Pearl
180 Harbor, and he was a darn good welder. Right after the bombing, he came to work but couldn't find his time card. The foreman told him he was no longer needed there. I read in the newspaper that Tom got plastic surgery on his eyelids, changed his name, then was arrested in San
185 Leandro after someone reported a 'Jap' on the street."

Phil drove slowly and continued, "The newspaper said the director of the American Civil Liberties Union[11] wants to use Tom's case to challenge whether it is even legal to put Japanese Americans in internment camps. The
190 director paid Tom's bail, but Tom went to the Tanforan internment camp anyway because his trial isn't until September. I may be one of Tom's only friends now. He said his people at the camp reject him too for trying to pass as White."

195 "It's good of you to write to him." I smiled, thinking of Sumi.

"He was a damn good welder."

We saw a short news film called *The Glamour Girls*. It showed women working in factories inspecting para-
200 chutes, going through machine parts on an assembly line, and driving buses. The narrator said, "There are over 300,000 women working in the aircraft industry now, but it's not enough. New workers are getting hired as soon as they apply. Even married women are signing up to go to
205 work. Working in a factory is no more difficult than housework. Instead of cutting the lines of a dress, this woman cuts the pattern of aircraft parts. Instead of baking

---

[11] The American Civil Liberties Union (ACLU) was created in 1920 and still exists today, working to protect people's constitutional rights.

a cake, she is cooking gears to reduce the tension of the parts after use. With a little training, a woman can learn to use a factory tool as easily as using her home tools, like her juicer or iron. When necessary, machinery is adapted for feminine muscles, like this lazy-arm drill, which takes the strain off. Women can do the same jobs as men and get the same pay. Gals, hoping won't bring him back sooner. Get a war job! See your United States Employment Service now!"

We settled in as the main film, *Casablanca*, started. From the corner of my eye, I saw Phil's arm creep around the back of my chair, and his fingers rested on my shoulder. I asked myself what I was doing in a movie theater with another man. I imagined Joe getting shot at as I pushed a handful of popcorn into my mouth.

By the end of the movie, I was wiping tears away. When the lights came on, Phil smiled at me and put his handkerchief in my lap.

Outside the winter air was still and calm. We were quiet on the ride home. Phil parked in front of my house and turned to face me. "The couple in the movie had that unbeatable chemistry that happens only once in a lifetime," he said.

My only response was to blush.

Phil opened the car door for me and we walked up the steps. He kissed me on the cheek and said, "I had a swell time. Thanks for coming out with me." Then he got into his car and drove off. I stood there, wishing he'd come back, still feeling guilty.

Chapter 10: Troubles

That weekend the kids helped me can a chicken and bake cookies to send to Joe. We saved the chicken fat to bring to the butcher shop, to make glycerin for explosives. I saved the broth for my lunches at work.

On Sunday evening, after the kids were in bed, I unfolded a letter from my sister, Diana. I lay on the sofa in my socks and read:

Dear Lolly:

I have plenty of time to write to you now because I am lying in bed with two broken legs. I was lettering the side of an airplane when some joker came along and moved my ladder. I fell 10 feet to the concrete. I couldn't prove who did it because no one saw. Before it happened, today at break time the gals and I were talking about how nasty the boys get. We guess they are mean because they got rejected when they tried to join the service, so they take it out on us.

A few of the gals came by and brought me some flowers. We agreed we're all going to watch out for each other now. Also, we're going to work even harder since it seems like the only way to get respect is to do a better job than the men.

Love, Diana

My God, I hope her legs recover, I thought. I sure knew what she meant by "nasty boys" at work.

In the locker room on Monday morning, Hattie told

me she had to go to the hospital to visit her brother. "There was a terrible accident," she said. "He was doing his job loading munitions and it all exploded."

30 "My God, was he hurt?"

"I don't know. I haven't seen him yet."

After work, on the way to the center to pick up the kids, I bought a newspaper with the headline "Port Chicago Explosion."[12] I sat on the curb and read it.

35

AT THE PORT CHICAGO NAVAL BASE ON SUISUN BAY, 320 MEN DIED AT A MUNITIONS SHIPMENT FACILITY, AND 390 PEOPLE WERE INJURED.

MUNITIONS WERE BEING LOADED ONTO SHIPS BOUND
40 FOR THE PACIFIC THEATER. CARGO INCLUDED BOMBS, SHELLS, NAVAL MINES, AND TORPEDOES. AFTER FOUR DAYS OF AROUND-THE-CLOCK LOADING OF 4,600 TONS OF EXPLOSIVES, THE SHIPS WERE 40 PERCENT FULL. SIXTEEN RAIL CARS STILL HELD MUNITIONS WAITING TO BE LOADED
45 ONTO SHIPS, WHEN A FULLY LOADED SHIP EXPLODED, CAUSING A HUGE FIREBALL THREE MILES IN DIAMETER. THE MAIDEN *SS QUINAULT* VICTORY SHIP, WHICH HAD BEEN RECENTLY DELIVERED FROM THE KAISER SHIP-YARDS, WAS TORN INTO SECTIONS AND THROWN IN MANY
50 DIRECTIONS. THE STERN LANDED UPSIDE DOWN IN THE WATER 500 FEET AWAY FROM THE DOCK. THE MEN LOADING THE SHIPS WERE KILLED INSTANTLY AND THEIR BODY PARTS WERE BLOWN FAR AND WIDE. A COAST GUARD FIREBOAT WAS THROWN 600 FEET UPRIVER,
55 WHERE IT SANK. CHUNKS OF GLOWING-HOT METAL AND BURNING WEAPONS WERE FLUNG OVER 12,000 FEET INTO THE AIR.

---

12 Port Chicago is in Suisun Bay, California, about 45 miles from San Francisco, and 30 miles from Richmond, where Lolly lives.

MANY NEARBY BUILDINGS WERE BADLY DAMAGED AND CIVILIANS AS WELL AS MILITARY WERE INJURED. THE
60 EXPLOSION WAS SO LOUD IT WAS HEARD IN THE CITY OF BERKELEY AND BROKE WINDOWS AT THE FAIRMONT HOTEL IN SAN FRANCISCO. THE CAUSE OF THE EXPLOSION IS STILL UNKNOWN, BUT AUTHORITIES ARE INVESTIGATING.

65   I folded the newspaper and whispered a prayer for Hattie's brother.

Stevedores loading munitions. Permission from the National Park Service from the collection of Port Chicago Naval Magazine National Memorial.

OFFICIAL PHOTOGRAPH
NOT TO BE RELEASED
FOR PUBLICATION
NAVY YARD MARE ISLAND, CALIF.

Naval barracks after the explosion. Permission from the National Park Service from the collection of Port Chicago Naval Magazine National Memorial.

After the explosion, Port Chicago. Permission from the National Park Service from the collection of Port Chicago Naval Magazine National Memorial.

That night at the center I asked Mrs. Ginzberg how Billy was doing with the toilet.

"I think we've made it over the hill, Mrs. O'Brien. He's fully toilet trained now," she said proudly.

70   I sighed with relief. "I've had no problems at home, either."

When I went into Billy's classroom, a teacher was playing the piano and singing, "My Country 'Tis of Thee." Billy sat cross-legged in the circle of children and 75   sang along.

In Edna's room, I watched her playing Ring Around the Rosie with the other girls. The children all seemed happy and engaged. I felt good about leaving them there.

Back home, after I tucked the children into bed, I 80   ironed some of their clothes for the week, then lay on the sofa to read a letter from Sumi.

My Dear Lolly:

It cheered me up to receive your letter and hear about your
85   *welding job. I'm also happy to say things are improving here. A library opened with 65 books, and I got a children's picture book to look at with Frankie. Last week we saw a movie in the racetrack grandstand called* Spring Parade.

Yesterday, over 5,000 people waited in line to be served a
90   *meal of sausages, two slices of bread, and a pitcher of tea for dinner. This was an especially good meal. We had protested earlier because we got liver for dinner three nights in a row. Before that it was beans and bread with no butter. At first everyone was hungry all the time, but now there is more food.*
95   *We use the dishes we brought from home and wash them ourselves.*

*The baby is due any day now. It may be crowded, a family of
four living in a 20x9 foot stall divided into two rooms, but a
family of six lives next to us in the same size stall.*

100   *My new friend Seiko had to sell her 26-room hotel for only
$500. She hid the money in a bar of soap because all our bank
accounts were frozen and we could only withdraw $100 before
coming here. Her five-year-old daughter got the measles and a
nurse came and took her away to keep the infection from
105   spreading. Poor Seiko didn't see her child for three weeks!*

      *Please write as often as possible. It cheers me up to hear
from you.*

      Your friend, Sumi

      P.S. Inside is a drawing I did.

110

      I unfolded the paper to find a detailed ink drawing of
her husband Hiroshi cutting the long grass growing
between the planks on the stable floor. Even though her
letter was cheerful, the drawing told the true story. At the
115   bottom of it she wrote, *The warping of the new lumber left
cracks in the floor an inch wide. The grass grew through the
cracks.*

Drawing by Mine Okubo, Tanforan horse stable, 1942
San Bruno, CA. Courtesy Seiko Buckingham

At lunch a few days later, I wanted someone intelligent to talk to, so I walked through the crowds at the shipyard to find Phil. I ignored the men's catcalls. I was so sick of their insults. I hated the way they looked at me, as if they were undressing me with their eyes.

I arrived in the lunchroom, got my food, and carried it over to a bench. Hearing a soft whistle, I looked up and saw Phil waving at me. He came over and sat down with me. I watched his handsome face as he talked.

"There's a dance Friday night. I haven't cut a rug in quite a while. Let's go, Lolly," he said. "Meet me at the canteen at 7:00 on Friday. See if the center can keep the kids overnight." Before I could refuse, he got up and walked off.

After work, I looked for Hattie in the break room. "How's your brother?" I asked.

"He's okay, but he has a broken wrist and he was acting awful strange, talking nonsense. I guess they gave him some medicine that makes him act funny. When the doctor told him he had to go back to work at the base, his face started twitching. He tried to talk the doctor into letting him stay at the hospital, which ain't like him, to argue with a White person. It's all over the newspapers. It was a terrible explosion. He must have seen his friends die." Hattie hung her head and looked down. Then she changed the subject. "I got another letter from my man. Can you read it to me?"

"Sure," I said.

Darling Hattie:

150 *I have lots of time to write you now because I am under arrest in my quarters, along with over a hundred other Negro officers.*

Here's the story: There are two officers' clubs here at the Freeman Field base. One is for the Whites and the other is for us. We call it Uncle Tom's Cabin[13] because it is so run down.
155 *Last night, a small group of us decided to go into the White officers' club. They told us only members could go in. We knew there were White officers in the club who were not members. I went past them to order a beer. The bartender said, "I can't serve you, you're not a member." I asked him, "How can you*
160 *tell?" He answered, "Because no Coloreds belong to the club."*

We refused to leave. Three of our men were arrested and put in jail. The rest of us are under house arrest. We knew that the official rule was that the buildings were open to all officers, no matter their race. We wanted to see if that was true.

165 *The general told the press that Freeman Field had two clubs; club number one for "trainees," and club number two for use by "instructors only." What he didn't tell the press was there are no Negro instructors. Many of our officers are qualified to be teachers, but are not allowed to be.*

170 *We are now charged with insubordination. We need strength to suffer all the insults. I wish the Whites would see that an integrated military could help win the war.*

Sweetheart, try not to worry about me. We continue to fight for the double victory: the war against racism here and the war
175 *for our country out there.*

Hattie, I was very happy to get your letter. I showed all my buddies your lipstick kiss at the end of it.

---

[13] *Uncle Tom's Cabin* is a famous book written in 1852 about slavery in the American South. An Uncle Tom's Cabin is a place in very bad condition.

Sorry to hear about your brother, Sam.

Your loving husband, Granger

180

Hattie took the letter from me, touched it with two fingers, then put it in her lunchbox. She looked off with an expression of hopelessness and mumbled, "Arrested..." Then she got up and walked out.

185

On the drive to the dance hall, I told Phil that I had gotten another letter from Sumi. "She had the baby. Her husband wrote that her labor lasted two days and they finally did a cesarean section to get the baby out. She
190 didn't get proper care during the operation, and the baby may not be healthy."

Phil looked straight ahead, his eyes on the road. "Let's pray for that family," he said.

"Yes, and that's not the only family to pray for.
195 Hattie's brother was in the Port Chicago explosion. She said they let him out early from the hospital so he could help clean up the shipyard mess and the bodies of the dead men. Hattie was pretty upset, and to make it worse, her husband was just arrested."

200 "That girl's got a load to carry."

We listened to the hum of the car motor as we sat in silence the rest of the way.

Slow dancing with Phil made me forget all the problems of the world. The dreamy music brought us
205 closer and closer together. When the band played "As Time Goes By," we kissed. The next song, "You Always

Hurt the One You Love," pulled me back to reality and we danced farther apart. Then we did a lively jitterbug and I told myself to enjoy it, since I never got to go dancing with Joe.

On the way back to my house, Phil reached over and held my hand as he drove. "I had a beautiful time with you, Lolly," he said.

At the door I gave him a little kiss on his cheek and started to go inside. He gently pulled my arm and said, "Aren't you going to ask me in for coffee?"

"Of course," I blushed.

Inside, I turned to put the water on for coffee, but before I could light the stove, he put his arms around me. My perfume and his cologne blended together as we floated into each other's arms.

Chapter 11: Joe's Visit

October brought much-needed rain. My little family got off the bus and splashed down the road in our rain boots, headed for home after a long day. Billy jumped from puddle to puddle yelling, "Sploosh!" I stopped
5   myself from scolding him as Mrs. Ginzberg's voice rang in my head, "Let children be children."

Reaching home, I retrieved the mail, put it on the kitchen table, and helped the children get into their nightclothes. After soup and toasted cheese sandwiches,
10 the children fell right to sleep. I opened the mail, saving Joe's letter for last. When I read it, my hands started shaking. He wrote that he had gotten leave, and would be home for Thanksgiving. I promised myself that I would end my love affair with Phil and chewed my fingernails.

15 Thanksgiving came faster than I expected, and before I knew it, we were waiting for Joe at the train station. The children were joyful as they watched all the excitement. Many soldiers got off the train, and there was a great deal of kissing and hugging when they found their loved ones.

20 Joe seemed taller and more muscular to me. He looked handsome in his Navy uniform. He kissed me, then noticed that Billy wasn't wearing diapers. "Looks like you've lost some weight, sport," he said.

During the bus ride home, I worried about how I
25 would explain our new dog. When we opened the front door, Fala ran to us, barked once, then rubbed himself on Joe's uniform.

Joe scratched the dog's head. "What's this little mutt doing here?"

30   Billy rolled a ball to Fala, and he brought it right back to him.

"What a smart dog," Joe said.

I heaved a sigh of relief that Joe didn't seem to be at all upset.

35   For our Thanksgiving meal, I made ground beef in the shape of a turkey using a recipe I had found in a magazine. With rationing, I couldn't find any real turkey in the market. I proudly put it on the table.

"The turkey's funny!" Edna laughed.

40   "That's a turkey?" Joe asked. "Very clever!"

After our big meal, I washed the dishes, and Joe surprised me by drying them.

"It's nice being a family again," I said.

"Isn't it bedtime for the kids yet?" Joe winked.

45   I put the children to bed and worried about sleeping with Joe. Would he know that I had been with another man? I took my time in the children's room until I heard his familiar call. Later, as my husband snored, I tried to remember the smell of Phil's aftershave.

50   The next morning after breakfast, Edna sat at the table with some crayons and paper while I did the dishes.

"Mommy, why did my teacher say I couldn't draw these?"

Joe and I looked at her drawing. It was a swastika.[14]

---

[14] The swastika is an ancient symbol that was used by Hitler's Nazi Party.

55   "Because, dear, that is a favorite symbol of the bad man who started the war."

"Oh." Edna's eyes got big as she balled up her drawing and threw it in the trash.

"Don't waste paper!" yelled Joe.

60   Edna looked confused.

"What teacher is she talking about, anyway?" Joe demanded to know.

"Honey, I got a war job. We needed the money, and they are recruiting everyone they can now," I said softly, 65 worried about Joe's reaction. "The children go to the Maritime Child Development Center while I am at work. It's a very nice place, a really good school," I said nervously.

"What's this war job you got?" His cigarette hung 70 from his mouth as he spoke.

"I'm a welder at the shipyard." My voice shook. I was confused, not knowing whether to feel proud or guilty.

Joe's eyes got big. "Why didn't you tell me?" He exhaled smoke from his cigarette. After a moment he 75 asked, "How much do you make?"

"I make a $1.30 per hour and I've even bought a few war bonds."

"Woooo!" Joe hooted. Then his eyes narrowed. "How many men do you work with?"

80   "Just some old 4F fellas, but mostly gals. The shipyard newsletter said we have 60 percent of the San Francisco symphony working there." I spoke fast, trying to reassure him so he wouldn't be jealous.

Joe got up and went into his workshop in the garage.

85 As I swept the kitchen floor, I thought about how much quieter our family was without Joe around.

The next day we went to Mass together. The children were better behaved than usual, enjoying us all being together. Other men there sat proudly in their uniforms
90 with their arms around their wives.

That night I asked Joe if he would watch the children the next day while I went to work. He was quiet for a minute, then asked me, "How much money did you say they pay you?"

95 When I came home from work the next day, Joe was sitting with Billy, drawing a ship and explaining all its parts. I kissed them both and sat down to rest my legs.

"The front of the ship is called the fore, and the back is the aft. Now, what's the main body called?" Joe said to
100 Billy.

Billy answered smartly in his little voice, "Hull."

"That's my boy. Someday maybe you'll be a sailor, just like your old man."

Joe's leave was almost over. Seven days had passed
105 quickly. When I saw how he loved and cared for our children, our marriage felt very important to me.

On his last day, Joe packed up his bag and we all took the bus to the train station. The children and I sadly watched the train pull away.

110 "Mommy, will Daddy come back?" Billy asked.

"Of course, when the war is over." I bent down and gave him a hug.

"When will the war be over?" Billy demanded.

"Nobody knows that, stupid!" Edna kicked a rock as

115 the last train car rolled away.

I bit my lip. I did not have the energy to discipline her. We all felt the loss.

—————   —————   —————

About a week later, Hattie seemed really worried at
120 break time.

"What's the matter, honey?" I asked her.

With a troubled face she explained, "It's my brother, Sam. He's locked away in prison now."

"Oh, Hattie. What happened?"

125 "They sent him back to work to clean up after the accident. But he stopped working when he saw a foot in a boot with no body attached. They made him leave the hospital before he was well. His roommate told me he's in solitary confinement now and I can't visit him there."

130 "That's terrible, Hattie. I'm so sorry." I put my arm around her as the back-to-work whistle blew. We got up from the bench and put on our gear.

After work, I got a newspaper to read more about the Port Chicago explosion. I unfolded it and read:

135

Port Chicago Mutiny

Fifty Negro men were imprisoned after refusing to do their jobs loading mines and other munitions on the *USS Sangay*. The men were taken under
140 guard to the Mare Island Naval Shipyard and imprisoned on a barge used as a temporary prison.

The next day when I saw Hattie at lunch, I told her I had read about the so-called mutiny[15] in the paper.

145 "Lord knows I have my troubles," she said, and sat down next to me, not even opening her lunchbox. "His friend Jim came by the room last night an' told me the whole story. Most of the sailors were afraid of loading the munitions after the explosion, especially after putting 150 body parts in wheelbarrows all day."

Hattie was so sad. I tried to cheer her up, but it was no use. She was stone quiet and walked right out of the break room while I was talking to her. Feeling helpless, I wished I could talk about it with Phil, but I didn't go 155 looking for him. With Joe's visit still fresh in my mind, I was determined to keep my wedding vows.

Later, during a break, I read a letter from my sister.

Dear Lolly:

160 *It took a while, but my legs have finally recovered. I'm writing this as I sit on the wing of a P-40 fighter during my break.*

This factory has a charm course I go to on Thursday nights. The instructor teaches us to be feminine even though we are 165 *doing men's work, and that factory work does not have to make us less womanly. We use a little blush on our cheeks and lips so we look pretty even while working. I read a magazine article that said we women should send our men a photo of ourselves in a swimsuit, to inspire the boys to keep fighting. A friend is* 170 *coming over this weekend to take a picture of me to "wow" my*

---

15 "Mutiny" means to break the law and go against authority. Calling it a mutiny, rather than a rebellion or uprising, made the men seem guilty.

Edwin. Maybe you should do the same for Joe!

My arms have been terribly sore because these rivet guns are so huge and heavy. I'll never feel helpless around the house again. I am so strong now. When I get home at night I'm usually so exhausted I fall asleep with my work clothes on.

A grinding wheel exploded in a woman's face here last month. It left a terrible scar. But she said it was her "badge of service for our country." I thought that was so brave of her.

I sure miss you, kid!

Love, Sis

Chapter 12: The Double War

I had not seen Phil for over two months. It wasn't easy staying away from him. I missed our intimate conversations. Of course, I couldn't talk to anyone about it, which made it even harder. Every day I brought my lunch from home in order to avoid seeing Phil in the canteen.

Hattie came into the break room and cheerfully announced, "I got a letter from my Granger. Will ya read it for me, Lolly?"

"I'd love to," I said, smiling.

Sweetie Pie,

I'm no longer imprisoned in the barracks in Indiana. We have been flown to Godman Field, Kentucky, because 101 of us men refused to sign a new base regulation that states that we can't use the White officers' club. One Negro officer signed and wrote, "This is racial discrimination."

The general put out a notice that said there would be strict segregation of base facilities and all the officers, Negro and White, were ordered to sign this new regulation. The Negro officers refused. We were then arrested and confined to our quarters. The next day, we were transferred under armed guard to Kentucky, where we were placed under house arrest again.

When we first arrived here, we were put in large prison vans that are used to transport German and Italian prisoners of war. When we got out, there were 75 military police armed with submachine guns. German POWs walked around without guards and seemed to be laughing at us, as if we were the enemy.

30 *We are still under house arrest with no work assignments, so we just play cards all day. We want to go back to Freeman Field and complete our combat training, then fly our planes overseas to prove that Negroes can play a big part in winning this war.*

35 *The general gave us a speech, saying, "This country is not ready or willing to accept a Colored officer as equal to a White one." He said that we are not in the U.S. Army to fight for our race, but to fight for our country." He ended his speech by adding, "We will not tolerate a mutiny and will find and remove racial agitators!"*

40 *I can't help wondering, at a time like this, isn't it more important for us to work together so we can successfully fight the war against the nation's enemy overseas?*

I sure do miss you, sweetie, and could really use your comfort at a time like this. Please write as soon as possible. Your
45 *letters keep me going.*

Your loving husband, Granger

"There's that nasty word, 'mutiny.' How can my husband and my brother both be using that word?"
50 Hattie said in a high voice as she sadly shook her head back and forth saying, "Uh-uh-uh..."

"I think it's important for Negro officers to fight for their freedom," I said. "I'm sure they've been feeling pretty useless not being allowed to go overseas into battle.
55 It must take a lot of strength to put up with those White officers."

Hattie took the letter from me. I could tell by her face that she didn't feel any better.

A few days later, I passed Phil on the way to the lunchroom.

"Please join me at the canteen for lunch," he said. "I just want to talk to you again."

"Okay, but just to talk," I said.

We got our food and sat down at a table together. I was so happy to see him again, and wanted to tell him everything.

"Sumi's baby is doing better and has gained weight, and Sumi recovered from the operation, thank God. I've been so worried about her. She wrote that the rain caused the track grounds to get soggy and sticky, like molasses, making it hard to get around. When it wasn't raining, the horseflies pestered them constantly. The wind was so cold and damp it blew right through the thin walls of the stable."

"It must be awful with a newborn in that environment," Phil said compassionately. "At least her husband is good to her. Go on, did she write any more?"

"She asked if I'd come see her."

"Really? I didn't know visitors were allowed."

"I was surprised too. No one under 16 is allowed."

"I'll watch your children for you," Phil offered.

"That's kind of you, but I'll take them to the child care center on Saturday and say I have to work. They love it there. On the weekend they get bored without other kids to play with, anyway."

"Our government should be ashamed of putting American citizens in camps like that," Phil said.

"When I read her letters, I get anxious, but she has a

strong faith that helps her stay positive. It makes me feel
90 grateful for what I have. I've been knitting a cap at night
for her baby."

Phil's eyes held mine. All the noise of the shipyard
disappeared. We were in a world of our own, just the two
of us in our closeness.

95 He broke the silence. "Let's go for a ride Wednesday
after work."

"I can't, Phil. I promised myself I'd be faithful." I
looked up at the gray ceiling.

"A short drive won't hurt."

100 "Talking is one thing, but I don't trust myself to be
alone with you." I looked down at my folded hands.

The whistle blew. Phil touched my shoulder and said,
"I'll pick you up at the canteen after work. Bring a picnic
dinner."

105 Before I could refuse, he was gone.

The ride to the ocean on Wednesday was full of colors.
Many shades of red, yellow, and blue filled our eyes as
the sun spread the last of its glory through the sky. With
110 all this beauty, it was hard to believe there was a war
raging out on this sea. From where we sat, the ocean
looked so peaceful, like it's name, Pacific. I had packed
extra food in my lunchbox and Phil brought a few bottles
of beer. He parked by a small cliff facing the ocean and
115 we spread out a blanket on the sand. We sat in silence
after we ate, and enjoyed being together as we listened to
the sound of the waves.

After a while Phil said, "I haven't had cornbread in a while. It was terrific."

120   "Thanks. It didn't turn out too bad without real butter. I never can find any. At least it has sugar."

Phil said, "I got a letter from my friend Tom. Remember I told you about him? He's Japanese American and worked at the shipyard with me."

125   "Yes, I remember. You told me he had gotten fired."

Phil wiped his mouth, tucked the napkin back in my lunchbox, and handed me a beer. "In the beginning of the letter it sounded like he was doing okay at the camp, and he even joined a group to help build a lake to beautify the
130   place. It was his idea to make a bridge and some islands."

I took a sip of my beer. "What else did he write?"

"He helped make toy sailboats for the kids to float in the lake."

"I wonder if little Frankie was there," I mused.

135   Phil shrugged, then continued, "He wrote that the men were angry after they walked around the racetrack on a hot day and saw a banner on a hillside outside the camp that read, ENJOY ACME BEER."

I swallowed wrong and started to hiccup, but
140   managed to say, "I guess they aren't allowed any beer in the camps. That must feel like a mean tease."

"I would think so. Also, he's trying to get copies of books in Japanese for his parents to read, but the guards won't allow it." Phil opened another bottle of beer for
145   himself, then looked over to see if I had finished mine. "A recruiting team came," he continued, "and they made all the men fill out a questionnaire for a volunteer combat unit."

150 "They're taking Japanese Americans into the service now from the camps?" I gasped.

"The questionnaire had 28 questions about their loyalty and willingness to fight. They forced everyone to fill it out, even his parents and sister." Phil glanced at my shocked face.

155 "Why did they do that?"

"I don't know. Tom wrote he was upset about two of the questions." Phil pushed another beer at me.

"What were they?" I anxiously drank more beer, even though it was quite bitter.

160 "Let's see...here it is." He reached into his pocket. "Hmmm," Phil said, running a finger down the letter. "Question 28: Will you swear unqualified allegiance to the United States of America and forswear any form of allegiance or obedience to the Japanese emperor or any 165 other foreign power or organization?'" Phil held the letter tightly. "His parents didn't want to give up their Japanese citizenship. If they did, they'd have no country to belong to. I can see their point."

I put my empty bottle in the sand as Phil handed me 170 another.

"This is the other question that Tom didn't like." Phil found the paragraph and read, "Question #27: Are you willing to serve in the Armed Forces of the United States on combat duty, wherever ordered?" Phil looked at me 175 intently. "Tom said everyone wanted to answer, 'I'll serve only if the camps are ended.' He said that anyone who wrote that or answered no was sent to a prison camp."

"Those poor people! I wonder how Sumi and Hiroshi filled it out?" I drank more beer and started feeling tipsy.

94

180   "Tom wants to join up just to get out of the camp, but is worried about leaving his family." Phil folded up the letter and frowned. "I'm patriotic, but what the government is doing to Japanese people makes me furious. Tom calls it 'guilt by ethnicity.'" Phil shook the

185   letter at me, adding, "I can't wait for this war to be over so they can have normal lives again. Has Hattie heard from her husband?"

    "I just read her a letter from him. It said all the Negro officers were released and can finish their training. They

190   hope to fly overseas into combat and help end this war."

    "That's a relief," Phil said, slugging down another beer.

    "Hattie was glad, but everyone got a permanent conviction in their file that said 'displayed a stubborn,

195   uncooperative attitude and lacks a sense of teamwork.'"

    "That's nasty!" Phil said.

    "I thought so, too. One of their men got convicted of pushing a White officer at the club and was reduced in rank and fined. This war has sure brought out the

200   ugliness as well as the heroism in people." I reached over and touched Phil's arm to soothe my anxiety.

    Phil's face brightened. "Let's get out and explore and forget about everybody's troubles. I have a flashlight."

    He helped me climb down the steep, narrow cliff as

205   the sun set and darkness came on. We felt the sand beneath our feet. I looked around. We were completely alone on the beach.

    His powerful flashlight shone on the cliffs, and he pointed it toward a narrow passageway. Phil left my side,

210   then jumped up and down joyfully like a child. "A cave! I

love caves!" He grabbed my hand and pulled me toward it. "Wow, Lolly, our own private cave!"

He held my hand as we made our way over sharp rocks, his flashlight guiding us. At last, his light fell on a
215 rocky passageway.

My voice echoed as I whispered, "It's warm in here." The salty ocean smell reminded me of adventure.

Farther inside, the cave got wider. At the back it was tall enough that we could stand up, but instead we fell
220 onto the sand in each other's arms as the waves broke against the rock walls of our cave.

Later, we listened to the sound of water drops falling from the roof of the cave. Phil moved the flashlight around and searched the sharp crannies above us.

225 Wishes circled around in my head: *I wish we could stay here forever, I wish I wasn't married...*

"I wish..." I started to say.

Phil put his finger on my mouth. "Hush. Let's forget all that, just for now."

Chapter 13: Life in an Internment Camp

"I got two letters. Can you read them for me?" Hattie asked me.

"Of course," I said.

"Read the one from my brother first."

5

Dear Hattie:

I asked my cellmate to write this for me so you know how I am doing and where I am.

10 *After we cleaned up our mates' bodies and the mess from the Port Chicago explosion, we were transported to another munitions ship on Mare Island. Fifty of us refused to do the work because they would not assure us that the munitions were not live. As a result, we were locked up and put in the brig.*

We also found out that many of the White officers were 15 *granted 30-day leaves to get away from all of the death. Not one Negro sailor was granted a leave, even though most of us asked for one.*

Before the explosion, the White officers told us we would be punished if we didn't load the munitions fast enough. Then they 20 *would race us, betting which group could load the fastest. When their superiors came by, they told us to slow down. We all think that the munitions <u>did</u> have live fuses, although we were told they did not.*

Admiral Wright told us that although loading ammunitions 25 *was dangerous, death by firing squad was even more dangerous. That's probably why many men are still loading munitions.*

I don't know what is going to happen to us. We are awaiting trial. I'd rather be here in this prison barge, because at least here I have some hope of staying alive.

30   *I've been having nightmares when the lights go out. I dream of the sound of the blast and of my friends screaming in pain. I see them dying, and I wake up covered in sweat.*

Please find someone to help you write back to me. Your letters calm me down.

35   *Your brother, Sam*

"Oh my God, Hattie, those officers were racing the sailors! No wonder there was an explosion!"

"Sweet Jesus, my poor brother! What would Mama
40   say?" Hattie shook her head. She held her face in her hands. A few minutes went by before she reached into her coveralls and pulled out a second letter. "Maybe this'll be better news."

I saw what she was holding and gasped. "Hattie,
45   that's not a letter; it's a telegram!"

"Dear Jesus, more trouble."

I grabbed it from her and read fast:

Western Union Telegram: I regret to inform you, your
50   *husband, Lieutenant Granger D. Calhoun, has been missing in action since 4 August. If further details or other information of his status are received, you will be promptly notified.*

Signed,

The Adjutant General

55 Hattie took the telegram from me, put her lunchbox in her locker, and walked out without a word.

The next Saturday, I kissed the children goodbye at the center and headed to the bus stop to go to Tanforan to visit Sumi. Standing in my welder's uniform, I watched 60 the busy street. The once quiet town was now bursting with people. It was so different from what it had been before the war that it seemed like a new town. There were people of many races, and an assortment of languages filled the air. It was exciting, but it sure was going to be 65 nice to get away from the city for a day.

On the bus I knitted and finished the pink cap for Sumi's baby. After about two hours, I looked out the window and saw a long line of people in front of a barbed wire fence. I guessed this was the place. Sure enough, the 70 bus driver yelled, "Tanforan." I hoped the line was not too long, since visiting was permitted for only two hours.

Motorists rolled down their windows and stared at the Japanese Americans behind the fence. Several yelled, "Look at the Japs!"

75 After the official inspection and an embarrassing search, I was pointed toward the grandstands. As I passed the guard towers, I saw guards pacing back and forth with rifles on their shoulders. I saw row upon row of horse stables. No wonder Sumi said that she got lost all 80 the time. In front of the stalls, lines of laundry blew in the light breeze of December. Beautiful, well-cared-for victory gardens were planted between the "barracks." I noticed hand-lettered signs on some of the stable doors. Some were darkly humorous, such as "Inner Sanctum," "Stall 85 Inn," and even "Scabiscuit." The famous race horse Seabiscuit had raced there in the 1930s; another reminder that these stables were now "homes."

I climbed high into the bleachers, and entered a large room filled with people hugging, crying, opening packages, and playing cards. Many of the Japanese Americans were knitting—young, old, female and male. One man in the corner was trying to play a flute above all the noise, and a lively game of craps was in progress.

Sumi and I found each other and embraced with the baby between us. I wiped the tears from my eyes. Sumi raised her voice above the crowd. "I missed you so much!"

"I missed you too. Your baby's beautiful! I knitted her a cap." I placed it on her small head, but she reached up and knocked it off. This made Sumi and me laugh. It felt good to be together again.

"Let's go outside so we can hear each other." Sumi put the baby's cap back on. "This grandstand room is wonderful. We've had talent shows, pageants, and dances in here. It really boosts everyone's morale." Sumi shifted the baby onto her other hip as the child stared at me.

I smiled and put my finger into her tiny hand and she held it tightly.

Sumi straightened out the cap. "Thanks for the hat. How did you find the time to come all the way here, what with working at the shipyard and taking care of your children?"

"It's an exhausting job, but the child development center provides meals to bring home after work, so I don't have to cook." I smiled at how cute her baby looked in the cap. "The food's not too bad, either. Can I hold the baby? You never told me her name."

Sumi passed the skinny little thing from her hip into my arms. "This is Eleanor."

120   "Cute name," I lied, and cuddled the baby. The Roosevelts didn't deserve Sumi's patriotic use of their names. "Where's Frankie?"

"At the new school. It's over there." Sumi pointed at a building, but they all looked the same to me.

125   I gazed out beyond the camp at the gorgeous view of the rolling hills of San Bruno, and noticed the beer sign that Phil had told me about.

"Frankie's new teacher, Miss Wakatsuki, used to teach in Berkeley. Thank the Lord our children get to go to
130   school here."

Eleanor started sucking on my hand. I laughed. "You funny little girl," I said, hugging her close.

There was construction going on everywhere, and loud hammering noises below us.

135   Sumi pointed. "Over there is one of the mess halls. It's hard to teach Frankie any manners, as everyone hurries through their meals. The children run and play around the dining hall instead of eating. Over there is one of the public bathhouses. The flush toilets are always broken.
140   Only half walls separate them. Some of us pinned up newspapers and set up boards for privacy. The showers are either too hot or too cold. The Army put chlorine foot basins in front of all the shower rooms for sanitation. Most of us avoid them."

145   "It sounds very primitive. I'm so sorry you have to stay here."

Sumi ignored my comment and continued, "That building with the flag near it, that's the post office." She waved her hand. "It's a busy place because all packages
150   have to be inspected. Over there are several churches."

"I'm glad you have churches," I said sadly.

"It's comforting to go to the services," Sumi said. "The store is in the middle, but there's usually nothing to buy. When there are things for sale, everyone goes and it's too crowded. Living here is all about lines. We have to line up for everything. Most of the time we order things we need from catalogs."

"How do you get money?"

"Well, at first we didn't get any, even for working full time, but now we get $8-$16 a month for full-time work, depending on the job," Sumi said quietly.

My mouth hung open as Sumi explained life in Tanforan. I could not stand to hear any more, but she wanted to tell me everything.

"Over there are the laundry buildings, where we can wash, dry, and iron our clothes. It's usually out of hot water and the boiler has blown up several times. Hiroshi and I trade off doing the wash after midnight, then we get a washtub and are guaranteed hot water."

"You have a wonderful husband. Where is he?" I tried to be upbeat and change the subject.

"He's off playing Goh or Shogi."

Sumi noticed my questioning face.

"That's chess and checkers. It keeps his mind off thinking about the store." Sumi gave Eleanor a pacifier to suck on, and hesitantly asked, "Lolly, I need a favor. I know you don't have much time."

"I'm glad to do anything for you," I said.

"I was hoping you could walk by our store and see if the Soleskys are keeping an eye on it."

"I could on my day off. I'll write and let you know how it is."

"Thanks. It would help us to know."

185 On the walk to her barracks, the smell of sewage filled the air. We went by row after row of horse stalls as Sumi read the numbers to find her way.

I tried to keep the conversation cheerful. "The gardens are beautiful. It looks like they get great care and attention."

190 "Yes, they do. Many of our people used to be gardeners and nurserymen."

We came to row number 207, "apartment" 58. It was semi-dark inside with only one window. A swinging half door, worn down by horses' teeth marks, divided the stall
195 into two rooms. Up above was open space that extended the full length of the stable. I heard snores, babies crying, people arguing, and even jitterbug music. The cracks and large knotholes in the walls didn't allow for much privacy.

200 There were three cots with straw mattresses. The beds were against a wall that was covered with dead insects on the whitewash. A hot plate sat on an old apple crate, plugged into the side of a single electric light bulb that hung from the ceiling in the middle of the stall.

205 Sumi watched my eyes pass over it all. "The first month was the hardest. Now at least the walls have been whitewashed. We were told we'd get linoleum soon to cover the grass. We threw lye down to get rid of the manure and urine smell, but it didn't help much."

210 The smell of manure was strong. I distracted myself from it by looking at Sumi's hand-painted pictures tacked

up on the walls. It showed the story of her internment. The first drawing was of Sumi and Hiroshi packing. In the next one, they were with other families, and all were carrying suitcases and wearing labels with numbers. One of the first paintings of the stall showed dirt on the floor with bugs and spider webs in the corners. Her last picture was precious, showing Frankie playing with other children in a clean, new classroom.

"Sumi, I can't believe how talented you are. I hope when you get out of here that you'll be able to keep painting."

"Thanks. I take classes here with a former professor of art from UC Berkeley, Chiura Obata.[16] There are 600 students of all ages, and 90 art classes to choose from. It gives me a sense of calm and order to paint."

I looked into her dark eyes and asked, "Tell me, Sumi, how are you doing, really?"

"I'm doing better than when we first got here and I was pregnant. I'm enjoying my new baby girl." Sumi touched Eleanor's cheek with her finger as the baby cooed. "There are improvements every day, plus I'm getting used to it."

I glanced around the confined stall and found that hard to believe. "I miss visiting you with my kids at your store," I said with tears in my eyes.

"I'm grateful to have a friend like you," Sumi whispered, her eyes tearing as she put her arm around my waist.

---

[16] Chiura Obata was a well-known Japanese-American artist and was on the faculty at UC Berkeley. While interned in the camps he helped create an art school there.

240   We strolled toward the exit of the camp. I reached out and hugged my friend tightly, holding back a flood of tears.

Sumi returned my affection, then moved away, mumbling, "I hope I will see you soon."

245   I sat in lonely sadness on the long bus ride home. The scenery outside the bus window was a blur as Sumi's life at Tanforan ran on through my mind.

Chapter 14: A New Barber Shop

I pushed the cart with my two children in tow. The walk to Sumi's store brought both sad and happy memories. I had been going to a store in the opposite direction of the Matsumotos' since their internment; that way the children wouldn't ask me questions about Sumi's family.

"I brought my jacks to play with Frankie!"Billy said as he skipped behind Edna and me.

"We aren't going to that store, stupid," Edna said with a know-it-all look on her face that matched her father's.

"Don't say that, Edna, it isn't very ladylike. Billy, I'm sorry; we're just checking on the Matsumotos' store, but they won't be there right now."

"Where are they? I want to see Frankie!" Billy wailed.

I tried to be patient. "They're in a different place, but they'll be back soon."

"Why did they move?" Edna yanked my skirt.

"Look, there's the store and the American flag." I rushed ahead.

Edna caught up to me and stood, staring. "Look at that striped pole in front of their store. What's that for?"

My mouth opened in surprise as I saw a new sign in the store window:

EARL RAY'S BARBER SHOP

25 "Let's go to the Soleskys. Maybe they have ice cream," I said, walking quickly down the block, away from the Matsumotos' store.

"I want chocolate," Billy sang out behind me.

We rounded the corner. I was glad to distract the
30 children away from the Matsumotos' store. We walked into Solesky's. I took a breath and politely said to the owner, "Hello, Mr. Solesky. How are you today?"

"Fine, thank you. What can I get for you?"

"Is there any ice cream available?"

35 "Just ice pops."

"I'll take two, and the newspaper."

With the children busy licking their sweets, I leaned toward Mr. Solesky and angrily whispered, "What happened to the Matsumotos' store?"

40 Mr. Solesky snapped, "Can't you see, lady? It's a barber shop now."

"Weren't you supposed to watch it until they got back?" My eyes narrowed.

He laughed. "You think they're coming back? It makes
45 more money as a barber shop than a vacant store, anyway." He got out a broom, sweeping away from us.

"Come on, children," I said angrily, pushing the cart furiously out the door and down the street as the children tried to keep up with me.

50

After the night in our cave, I went back to meeting Phil once a week at the canteen. We continued to share news about the social war raging here in our own country.

"Have you heard from Sumi?" Phil's asked.

55 "Her family has relocated to a camp in Topaz, Utah." I took a bite of my stew from last night's leftovers.

"What did she say that was like? I hear there are 16 Japanese detention camps in the U.S. now, all in states far inland. I'm waiting to hear from Tom to see whether he

60 has moved."

"She said everyone had smiles on their faces as they left the racetrack. But the train ride to Utah sounded like a nightmare." I looked away from Phil, trying to find the energy to tell him about it.

65 "Why, what happened?"

"She wrote that the train ride with the kids was difficult because all the shades were kept down so people from the outside couldn't look in. Plus the lights weren't working, so they could hardly see, and it was too hot.

70 Also, at one stop someone threw a brick through a window even though there were armed guards at each exit." I tried to eat my lunch and avoided Phil's eyes. "She said the trip took three days. Lots of children got sick, including hers, from the overheated train."

75 "I hope the new camp at least will be better than the last," he said, offering me a cookie.

I shook my head no to the cookie. "I've had bad news about Hattie. She got a telegram. Her husband's missing in action."

80 Phil looked into my eyes. "Don't worry, Lolly, they'll find him. There's the whistle. Let's go to the ship launching. It'll keep our minds off all these problems."

There must have been over 5,000 people on the deck of
85   the *SS Red Oak*. I proudly stood with my hand over my
heart and we all said the Pledge of Allegiance. A huge
American flag flew in the breeze. It was a glorious
occasion. The ship was finished and ready to sail. I looked
around and saw Chinese, Poles, Czechoslovakians,
90   French, Norwegians, Scottish, Irish, English, and Italians,
all of them American citizens. A gust of wind swept
across the bay, blowing some of the workers' caps off.

The actress Dinah Shore broke a bottle of champagne
on the bow as we all cheered. The reporters' cameras
95   clicked wildly. It was a proud day for us all.

Phil took a piece of confetti out of my hair. "What
shipyard will you work in next?"

"Yard two. I'll be working on the *SS Robert E. Peary*."

"The *Peary!* I heard they will try to build that in record
100   time. You will have to beat the current record of 10 days.
You may find yourself working a lot of overtime."

"I'll do my best. Don't you know there's a war goin'
on?" I said with a wink.

Phil laughed. "The first Liberty Ship built was the *SS*
105   *Patrick Henry*. It took 70 days to build in 1941. Most ships
now take 60 days. Hey, since you're off work early, let's
go to dinner in town before you pick up your kids."

Later, at the restaurant, Phil read me a letter he received
from his friend Tom.

110   *Dear Phil:*

We have all been relocated from Tanforan. We were tagged like luggage and sent to Topaz, Utah, way out in a dusty desert. On the long trip there, I saw nothing but alfalfa. Miles and miles of it. A rumor went around the train that we would all be
115   *bombed to death when we got to Topaz. But on our arrival we were surprised to hear a Japanese band of former Boy Scouts, who welcomed us with songs. Then I noticed the barbed wire, the guards in towers, and hundreds of black tar-papered military barracks and I knew once again we were prisoners in*
120   *our own country. Then we were put into holding pens, like animals.*

Everyone is dusty and dirty. The dust blows through the cracks in the unfinished barracks where we sleep. We wear scarves over our faces, even inside. Please write. It's nice to
125   *have letters from the "outside."*

Your friend, Tom

"Gosh, Phil, it's so depressing. When will this war end?" I said hopelessly. "Sumi's store was sold behind
130   her back."

"How the hell can that be legal?" Phil stirred his coffee fiercely.

That night at home I listened to the news broadcast.

"Dillon Myer, National Director of the War Relocation
135   *Authority, stated to the press today, 'There are approximately 40,000 young people below the age of 20 years old in the Japanese relocation centers. It is not the American way to have children growing up behind barbed wire and armed guards.'"*

"Then why do they continue to build more internment
140   camps?" I mumbled to myself, in a dark mood.

A few days later, I ran into Hattie on the *SS Peary*. She was not her usual cheerful self. I could tell she was worried about her missing husband, and her brother in prison.

145 We clamped on the ground cable from a Lincoln generator, and dragged the cables around all day. We leaned and kneeled, trying to keep up the pace and make a record for shipbuilding. I moved my stinger back and forth, making rows and rows of shiny dots. I was

150 becoming a good welder. I could burn rod with the best of them.

During break time, Hattie said, "I'm glad we're still working together. I got a letter from Sam. Can you read it for me?"

155 "Sure. Have you heard from your husband?"

Her downcast face gave me the answer as she slowly said, "No," then handed me the letter from Sam.

Dear Hattie:

160 *Fifty of us went to court and were charged with mutiny. We have been reduced in rank and given 15 years hard labor. I am now in prison on Terminal Island in San Pedro Bay. I did the best I could to serve my country, but look at where I ended up. I hope you can find someone to help you write to me because you*

165 *are my only connection with the outside world.*

Your Brother, Sam

I felt like crying as I looked at Hattie's downturned face and tight lips. "I'll write a letter for you," I said

170 quietly.

She stood up slowly, her face like a mask, and said, "Thanks, maybe tomorrow." I saw tears rolling down her face as she left the room.

175   When we finally welded the last pieces of the ship together, everyone cheered. Our foreman announced, "We broke the record. We built the *Peary* in four days!"

But Hattie wasn't cheering.

180   One night the following month, after I got the children to sleep, I went through the newspaper to find news about Port Chicago. It wasn't in the headlines; I found it buried in the back of the paper.

PORT CHICAGO MUTINY: NEGRO
185   ### SAILORS FACE TRIAL

ON JULY 17, IN PORT CHICAGO, CONTRA COSTA COUNTY, ON THE SOUTHERN BANKS OF SUISUN BAY, TWO SHIPS, THE SS O'BRIEN AND SS QUINAULT BLEW UP DURING MUNITIONS LOADING. THE EXPLOSION IS THE WORST
190   DISASTER AT HOME SINCE THE WAR BEGAN.

THE SURVIVING SAILORS WERE RELOCATED TO MARE ISLAND TO CONTINUE THEIR WORK. FIFTY NEGRO SEAMEN REFUSED TO WORK AND WERE PUT IN THE BRIG. THE SAILORS PLEADED NOT GUILTY. THE TRIAL, KNOWN AS THE
195   PORT CHICAGO MUTINY, LASTED FOR OVER FIVE WEEKS.

DURING THE TRIAL THESE FACTS CAME OUT: THE POWERED WINCHES FOR LOADING WERE OLD AND WORN DOWN. THE TRAINING CENTER FOR WORKERS TO LEARN HOW TO LOAD MUNITIONS WAS NEVER USED. THE
200   MUNITIONS WERE PACKED VERY TIGHTLY AND WERE DIFFICULT TO GET OUT OF THE RAIL CARS. MANY OF THE

SHELLS WERE DAMAGED AND LEAKED BEFORE THE EXPLOSION. THE SEAMEN HAD BEEN TOLD THAT THE MUNITIONS WERE NOT ACTIVE SO THEY COULD NOT EXPLODE, AND THAT THE FUSES WOULD BE ADDED WHEN THEY ARRIVED AT THEIR DESTINATIONS. BUT IN FACT, MANY OF THE MUNITIONS WERE LIVE. ANOTHER FACT THAT CAME OUT WAS THAT ONLY NEGRO SAILORS WERE LOADING MUNITIONS. IN ADDITION, WHITE OFFICERS FORCED NEGRO LOADERS TO RACE EACH OTHER WHILE LOADING THE MUNITIONS.

THE NATIONAL ASSOCIATION FOR THE ADVANCEMENT OF COLORED PEOPLE FOUND THAT THE NEGRO SAILORS WERE NEVER PERMITTED TO ADVANCE IN RANK. THEY ALSO NOTED THAT THE WHITE OFFICERS WERE GRANTED SURVIVORS' LEAVE AFTER THE EXPLOSION AND THE NEGRO SAILORS WERE NOT. THE FINAL VERDICT STATED THAT 208 NEGRO SAILORS WERE CONVICTED OF DISOBEYING ORDERS, AND EACH LOST THREE MONTHS' PAY.

FIFTY OF THE DEFENDANTS WERE FOUND GUILTY OF MUTINY AND WERE REDUCED IN RANK TO SEAMAN APPRENTICE AND SENTENCED TO 15 YEARS OF HARD LABOR FOLLOWED BY DISHONORABLE DISCHARGE.

I sadly put down the paper and turned on the radio.

"A record-breaking Liberty Ship was assembled in four days, 15 hours, and 29 minutes at the Kaiser Shipyards in Richmond, and was named the SS Robert E. Peary, *after an American Arctic explorer.*

"Yard number two won the competition for speed in this amazing act. The ship will go to war in 10 days and carry 17 U.S. Naval Armed Guards with 43 Merchant Mariners. Congratulations, Ship Yard Two!"

I felt proud to read about the ship I had helped build. Exhausted, I fell asleep on the couch. "On to the next ship!" I shouted out in a dream.

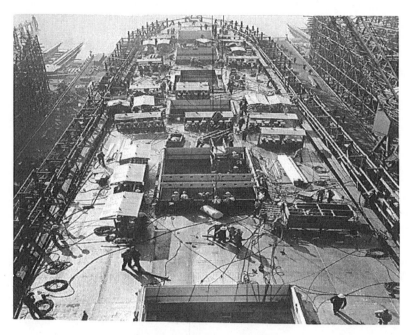

The completed Marin ship

Chapter 15: An Army of Americans

When I met Phil at the canteen the next day, I told him all about the Port Chicago Mutiny.

Phil shook his fist. "The Negroes and Japanese Americans have their own wars to fight right here on the home front. That reminds me, I got a letter from Tom. He joined up."

"They're really letting Japanese Americans fight in the war?"

Phil nodded. "The war is lasting so long the government is desperate for more soldiers."

"Does this mean the internment will end for them?"

"I'm afraid not."

"When Tom's on leave, he has to go back to the camp?"

"It's hard to believe, but I guess so. I'll read you his letter; it's a long one." Phil reached into his shirt pocket and slowly pulled it out, like it was a piece of heavy metal from the shipyard.

Dear Phil:

After a group of us petitioned the government to join the U.S. Army, I signed up. They wanted 1,500 volunteer Nisei (Japanese born in the U.S.) and over 10,000 volunteered. We are no longer classified as 4C, enemy aliens. Many of us volunteered with the hope that maybe they would release our families sooner. Joining up was the only way I could show my loyalty to the U.S. I am concerned about leaving my parents, but the other Japanese Americans at the camp in Topaz will take care of them.

30   I am now in the 442ⁿᵈ Army Battalion, which joined with the 100ᵗʰ Battalion from Hawaii. We do not get along. Those Hawaiian Japanese dress and talk just crazy. When they are not in uniform they wear bright, colorful shirts and necklaces made of flowers. They go barefoot all the time and hate wearing boots.
35   They call us "stuck-up" and we call them "buddaheads." That's from the Japanese word "buta," meaning "pig." So they call us "kotonks," after the sound of an empty coconut falling on the ground or like a head hitting a wall during a fist fight.

        The hostility between our two groups got really bad. There
40   were fist fights and lots of name calling. The White officers asked us how we were going to get along overseas in battle if we couldn't get along during basic training in Mississippi. To solve this problem, we were all brought on a trip to Jerome, a nearby internment camp in Arkansas. On the way, the
45   mainlanders stayed on different sides of the buses from the Hawaiians, who were playing their guitars and ukuleles. But as soon as they saw the barbed wired fences with White guards pointing machine guns at Japanese families, they got real quiet. They were humbled again when they learned that interned
50   families had saved a week's rations just to throw a party for us enlisted men.

        In Hawaii, only a small group of Japanese people were interned. It was nowhere near the numbers on the mainland. They were going to send all the people of Japanese descent to a
55   nearby island called Molokai, but it never happened. They would have lost one-third of the population of Hawaii if they had. Besides, they needed people to rebuild Pearl Harbor after the bombing.

        On the way back to the barracks in Mississippi, we all had a

60 *calm talk about the internment camps. We get along well now since they see the heartbreak we have gone through.*

We are all trained and ready to fight now, but they still haven't sent us overseas. We can't prove our loyalty until we fight, so I hope they send us soon.

65 *Your friend, Tom*

Japanese-American soldiers

"I can't believe that they're taking Japanese Americans out of the camps and training them to be soldiers without ending the internment," I said. "I hope Hiroshi doesn't
70 join up and leave Sumi all alone. The letter I just got from her didn't mention him, but she wrote about a terrible incident at Topaz."

"What happened?" Phil asked.

"A friend of hers, an elderly man, was shot to death at
75 the camp."

"My God! How did that happen? I thought the camps were peaceful places."

"She wrote that the military police on duty said he was too close to the fence and they warned the man to
80 move. When he didn't move back, the guard shot and killed him. Turns out, he was deaf."

"Shhooot!" Phil exclaimed. "From what I know about Topaz, even if you could escape, there would be nowhere to go. It's just desert for miles and miles."

85

From the 125-amp Lincoln generator, I clamped the ground cable to a sheet of metal, took the stinger, and selected the right number rod from the box. My arms hurt from pulling the cables around, and my knees swelled
90 from all the kneeling and leaning.

Hattie rushed in, waving a letter. "Lolly, Lolly I do believe this is a letter from my Granger!"

"Thank the Lord," I said, dropping my equipment and snatching it from her. I read it out loud.

95 *Sweetie Pie:*

I am alive! The Army said they sent you a telegram that I was missing.

I was on a flying mission escorting a White bomber crew when my plane was shot down over Belgrade. That's a city in
100 *Eastern Europe.*

I was flying my red-tail P-51 Mustang when I went down. I managed to parachute out and land in a garden. After I landed, a teenager with a pistol came up to me and said, "Hello." It turns out it was the only English word he knew. He
105 *looked real surprised, like he had never seen a Negro before. But when he saw the insignia on my uniform he smiled, so I knew he knew we were allies.*

The boy helped me hide in a two-wheel cart under some straw. For 39 days his family kept me hidden from the Nazis.
110 *They moved me from one barn to another. They fed me, gave me blankets, and even took me to a barbershop to get my hair cut. Eventually they brought me together with 11 other downed pilots and we went right back out flying missions.*

We are a proud group. All the White pilots ask for us
115 *because we haven't lost a bomber yet. Our all-Negro 332nd Fighter Squadron painted our 72 bombers bright red so the White bomber crews can follow us as we escort them to safety. They know we would give our lives for our country.*

So, we continue to fight for the "Double V": victory over
120 *Hitler overseas and victory over racism in America.*

Honey babe, I can't begin to tell you how much I miss you. Please keep me in your prayers.

Your Lovin' Husband, Granger

Hattie's eyes filled with tears. I felt her burden release as I held her in my arms. She let loose, her body shaking. I could hardly keep from crying myself, and thought how much she deserved this good news.

Tuskegee Airman

It was a cold night, January 2nd, 1945. From the news, it sounded like this might be the year the war would end. I was stretched out on the bed, listening to a radio broadcast.

"Today the Japanese-American exclusion order was rescinded. The Supreme Court ruled in December that detainment of loyal citizens is unconstitutional. Detainees are now free to go. Each will receive $25 and a train ticket home."

"Hooray!" I yelled. Then I thought about Sumi, and my cheerfulness died.

The next day at lunch, Phil handed me a letter from his friend Tom. "At least the war on the home front is over," he said.

I raised my eyebrows, but said nothing.

Dear Phil:

I am glad to receive your letters. They keep me going.

Recently, our 442nd regiment joined the 100th regiment in Northern Italy. We surrounded the Germans and in one afternoon forced them to surrender. For that we were awarded the highest honor, a presidential citation.

Then, with only one day of rest, we received orders to rescue the 141st, known as "the lost battalion of Texans." The Germans had them surrounded, and they had gone without food and water for seven days. They sure looked surprised to see us short Japanese guys rescuing them from the Nazis!

We rescued the 211 Texans, but 216 of our people died, and 856 of us were wounded. When the general got us all together to receive our awards, he said, "I want <u>all</u> the men here." Our *commanding officer responded, "General, these are all the men that are left."*

160   *The Army now calls us the "Christmas Tree Regiment," because we received so many decorations and awards. We continue to try to break every Army record there is.*

    Your Friend, Tom

165   "The patriotism of the Japanese-American soldiers is unbelievable," Phil said warmly. "The newspapers reported that for weeks our White troops tried and failed to rescue the Texans. Tom's battalion had the will to rescue them, but they sure paid for it."

170   I looked off into the distance as the clouds began to build up.

    "Well, at least our country honored the Japanese-American soldiers that survived," Phil added. "Have you heard from Sumi yet? Is she back?"

175   I couldn't look at Phil as I whispered, "I got a very upsetting letter from her last week. Her husband volunteered for the Army and was killed rescuing the Texans." I blinked several times, then I couldn't control myself any longer and cried into my hands.

180   Phil took out his handkerchief and gently patted my face. He put his arm around me as I buried my face in his shoulder.

    "Sumi is staying at Topaz, even though she could leave. She doesn't have the strength to start over, being a
185 widow with two young children."

    "They're keeping the internment camps open?"

    "At least for a while, I guess."

The 442nd "Christmas Tree" Army regiment

Chapter 16: Victory and Loss

Victory in Europe finally came, followed by the news of the two atomic bombs dropped on Japan. It was just a matter of time until the war ended.

As I entered the shipyard on a hot August morning, I sensed something different in the air. I had a bad feeling at the bottom of my stomach. A foreman guarded the stairs to the ship, blocking the women's entrance. "We don't need ya now, girls. Our boys are on their way home and are ready to work. The war is over. You can all go back to your kitchens."

I looked at the women. Everyone had the same lost, sad look on their face.

A coworker, Roslyn, cried with great sobs. "My husband ain't comin' back. I'm a widow now. How am I gonna support my kids?"

No one spoke as we slowly left the Kaiser Shipyard for the last time.

Phil caught me outside the yard, lifted me up, and swung me around. "It's over! It's finally over! We won the war!"

My sadness over Roslyn's troubles and my job ending faded away as the news finally began to sink in. The war was over!

Phil said, "My mother went to visit her sister. Why don't you come over to the house?"

"I don't think so. Joe wrote me that he'll be home in a few days."

"Then it will be our last time together. Like I promised, I'll let you go when your husband comes back." He tried to lead me toward his car, but I stood firmly on the pavement.

He ignored my stubbornness and opened the passenger's door. "Come, sweetheart," he said.

As I looked at him, I lost my resolve and got into his car.

"Let's drive to downtown San Francisco first to see the celebrations."

We rolled our windows down and enjoyed the warm summer breeze.

"I got a letter from Tom, probably the last. It was written a few months ago," Phil said as we rode down the highway.

"I wondered if his battalion was involved in the final part of the war." I stretched out my arm and moved my fingers through the wind.

"As a matter of fact, the 442nd helped liberate people from the concentration camp in Dachau."[17]

"It must have been frightening to see a concentration camp."

"It's ironic that when he returned to the States, he was released with his family from their camp."

---

[17] Millions of people, mostly Jews, were imprisoned in concentration camps in Europe during World War II. From 15-20 million people died in the camps. About six million Jewish people, about half the Jewish population at the time, were killed in Europe during the war.

As we turned onto Market Street in San Francisco, all traffic stopped. The street was filled with people, all kissing, hugging, and shouting. We turned off the car and heard horns, sirens, and whistles. Women and children rode on men's shoulders. Sailors were everywhere, throwing their hats into the air, hollering, leaping with joy, and drinking beer.

We made our way to Phil's neighborhood in Russian Hill. Children did somersaults on their lawns, and women banged on pots. Church bells rang all over the city.

Phil's house was cozy and clean. He kissed me in the middle of the living room, but I stepped away from him.

He said, "Lolly, I love you so much, but I'll keep my promise, this will be the last time."

Then I let go and embraced him. Knowing the affair had to end set a fire burning in our hearts.

Meeting Joe at the train station was awkward for the children, as they hadn't seen their father in almost two years. My cross and my wedding band had been put away for a long time, and now felt cold against my skin. Joe rushed off the train through the crowds of soldiers and hugged me tightly. I tried not to stiffen. He picked up the children, but they shyly leaned away from him.

Within days Joe got his old job back at the trucking company. After work, he would greet us gruffly and light up a cigarette. It was just like old times, I thought sadly. With his raise in pay he bought a new Motorola radio that fit neatly on a table in front of his rocker. It blared:

"At the Ford Plant in Michigan, women are carrying signs saying: 'Stop discrimination against women' and 'Why no work for women?' Ladies, the shipyard gold rush is over!"[18]

85 From the kitchen I heard Joe mumble, "Dames belong at home with their husbands. How dare they try to take jobs away from our boys coming home from the war?"

I didn't have the strength to argue with him. But I thought about the two widows I knew, Sumi and Roslyn, 90 and wondered how they were getting by.

After Joe went into the garage, I sat in the living room and read a letter from Diana, who was pregnant now.

Dear Sis,

95 *I'm glad not to be working anymore. I bet you are too. Edwin got a job in the city as a manager of a zinc company. We bought a three-bedroom house on Long Island with help from the VA bill. I'm getting rounder and rounder every day and we have an adorable bassinet just waiting for our precious package.* 100 *Has Joe bought a television yet? It's all the rage. I love mine!*

Write soon,

Love, Sis

"I'm Dreaming of a White Christmas" played on the 105 radio as I read a Popeye comic book to Billy. I skipped over the part that said, "Let's blast 'em Japanazis!"

Edna came in holding her roller skates. "Mommy, can you show me how to put these on?"

---

[18] Women had gotten used to working and earning their own income during the war. After it ended, even unmarried and widowed women could no longer find well-paying jobs.

Joe, full of the Christmas spirit, said, "Come on outside with me, babycakes, I'll teach you how."

Billy and I went out with them. Joe placed one of the skates on Edna's shoe. He pushed the ends of the skate together and tightened it with a key, then put the other one on. Edna weaved and tilted at first, but she soon glided confidently along the sidewalk as we all clapped. Billy ran in and grabbed his new silver steel coil spring toy called a "Slinky." Joe showed him how to make it "walk" down the front steps.

I left Joe outside with the children and went inside to enjoy some quiet time. I picked up the *Ladies Home Journal* and read an article titled "What Men Want."

MEN WANT THE WOMEN OF THEIR DREAMS IN THE KITCHEN. GIRLS, IF YOU WANT TO BE A DOCTOR OR A LAWYER—MARRY ONE! PURSUE A "MRS. DEGREE" OR A PH.T., "PUTTING HUBBY THROUGH." GIRLS, YOU CAN'T HAVE A CAREER AND BE A GOOD HOUSEWIFE AND MOTHER. TO KEEP BUSY WHILE YOUR HUSBAND WORKS, JOIN A CHURCH CLUB, THE PTA, OR A SCOUT GROUP. DOING SO WILL HELP YOUR MARRIAGE!

After Christmas vacation, Edna came home from school one day with a letter. I read it out loud:

Our class has read the story of Sadako Sasaki, a Japanese girl who survived the atomic bomb in Hiroshima. The bomb poisoned her with a disease called leukemia. A Japanese legend says that if you fold 1,000 white cranes from Origami paper you will be given a wish. Sadako wished for world peace and started folding cranes. She had folded 644 cranes when she died at age 12.

A sculpture was built for her. It shows Sadako on top of a mountain with her arms raised high, a crane in her hand. This prayer is carved on the stone:

145

This is our cry

This is our prayer

Peace on Earth

Please make as many cranes as you can with your child to send to school, and we will mail them to Japan along with
150 *thousands of Origami cranes that people are sending from all over the world.*

Together, Edna and Billy and I studied the diagram from the teacher and folded many cranes. I wondered
155 how so much death and destruction could motivate people to such acts of cooperation and productivity as this. I had helped build an entire ship in four days. I wondered whether someday peace could become the motivating force to bring people together, instead of war.

160

I walked out to get the mail as Fala followed behind. He watched me as I reached inside the box. Sumi was on my mind, but I couldn't see her now. Joe wouldn't like it, and peace in my family was my top priority since there
165 was a new baby on the way. I only hoped that the baby had blue eyes like we had, and not brown like Phil's.

A familiar Model A drove slowly by. I closed the mailbox and quickly turned back toward the house. Fala's pointed ears pricked up as I softly hummed a line of the
170 song from *Casablanca*, "A sigh is just a sigh..."

History

History of the Japanese-American Internment

1/14/42: Presidential proclamation required all aliens to report any change of address, employment, or name to the FBI. Enemy aliens were not allowed to enter restricted areas. Violators of these regulations were subject to arrest, detention, and internment for the duration of the war.

Executive Order 9066, 2/21/42: Authorized the Secretary of War to prescribe military areas (the entire West Coast and Southern Arizona) from which any or all persons were to be excluded to protect against espionage and sabotage.

Military commanders enforced compliance. The Secretary of War was authorized to provide for the residents of military areas: transportation, food, clothing, shelter, use of land, shelter supplies, equipment, utilities, facilities, medical aid, hospitalization, and other services as necessary. The Federal Bureau of Investigation would investigate alleged acts of sabotage.

Public Proclamation No. 1, 3/2/42: Anyone having "enemy" ancestry had to file a change of residence notice if they moved.

Executive Order 9095, 3/11/42: Created the Office of the Alien Property Custodian, which had authority over all alien property interests. All assets were frozen.

3/24/42 Public Proclamation No. 3: Declared a curfew (6:00 a.m. - 8:00 p.m.) for all enemy aliens and persons of Japanese ancestry within the military areas.

5/3/42: Civilian Exclusion Order No. 34: General DeWitt ordered all people of Japanese ancestry, whether citizens or noncitizens, in Military Area No. 1 (West Coast) to report to "assembly centers" where they would live until moved to permanent "relocation centers."

Between 110,000-120,000 people of Japanese ancestry were subject to this mass relocation program, two-thirds of whom were U.S. citizens.

Eighteen Temporary Civilian Assembly Centers were used to house the Nisei (Japanese Americans) and Issei (Japanese citizens living in the U.S.A.): racetracks, stables, migrant workers' camps, Civilian Conservation Corps camps, county fairgrounds, and warehouses. They were located in California, Arizona, Washington, and Oregon.

Permanent Internment Camps built: Ten in Arizona, Colorado, Wyoming, Arkansas, California, Idaho, and Utah.

Justice Department detention camps: There were eight that held German and Italian detainees in addition to Japanese Nisei and Issei. They were located in Texas, North Dakota, Montana, New Mexico, and Idaho.

Citizen Isolation Centers for problem inmates: There were three located in Arizona, Utah, and New Mexico.

Federal Bureau of Prisons for detainees convicted of crimes: There were three camps, located in Arizona, Kansas, and Washington.

United States Army Facilities held German, Italian, Issei, and Nisei detainees. There were 18 located in California, Florida, Louisiana, New Mexico, Wisconsin, Arizona, Maryland, Oklahoma, and Hawaii.

There were 11,507 people of German ancestry and

10,000 people of Italian ancestry who were interned and evacuated from the military areas.

Only Hawaiians of heightened perceived risk (1,200-1,800 of Japanese ancestry) were interned.

Many internees were temporarily released from their camps to harvest crops due to the wartime shortage of labor.

National Student Council Relocation Program: students of college age were permitted to leave the camps (2,263) to attend institutions willing to accept students of Japanese ancestry.

There were Japanese Americans who remained in their own homes and were not evacuated if they were living in the Midwest, East, or South.

Statement of United States Citizen of Japanese Ancestry (loyalty questionnaire) 1/23/43: No. 27 and No. 28 were the most controversial.

- **No. 27:** Are you willing to serve in the Armed Forces of the United States on combat duty wherever ordered?
- **No. 28:** Will you swear unqualified allegiance to the United States of America and faithfully defend the United States from any or all attack by foreign or domestic forces, and forswear any form of allegiance or to the Japanese emperor, to any other foreign power or organization?

Percentage of people who answered question #28 of the loyalty questionnaire positively: 89.4.

Number of internees who answered negatively to question #28: 5,589. They renounced their U.S. citizenship and were sent to the Tule Lake High-Security Segregation Internment Camp.

The **Tanforan Temporary Assembly Center** in San Bruno, California, 4/42-10/42 had 7,800 Bay Area people of Japanese descent.

California State Historic Landmark #934, Tanforan Racetrack Japanese Assembly Center, Tanforan Park Shopping Center on El Camino Real, San Bruno reads: "Racetrack opened in 1899 and had racing seasons until it burned down in 1964. Many famous horses raced and won here. In 1942, Tanforan became a temporary assembly center for over 4,000 persons of Japanese ancestry who were to be interned for the duration of World War II."

Topaz Permanent Internment Camp, Millard County, Utah, 140 miles south of Salt Lake City, 19,800 acres. Peak population: 8,130, 9/11/42-10/31/45. Temperatures: 106 degrees in summer to -30 degrees in winter, frequent dust storms from constant wind.

James Hatsuki Wakasa walked near the internment fence, did not hear the sentry's warning, and was shot to death on 4/11/43.

Toyosaburo Fred Korematsu: 1/30/19-3/30/05, born in Oakland, California. Lost his job at Kaiser Shipyard after the bombing of Pearl Harbor because of his ancestry. When Executive Order 9066 was issued, he became a fugitive, changed his name on his identification card and was arrested for evading internment (breaking Public Law 503, enemy alien staying in a military area) and put in jail. While incarcerated, an attorney from the American Civil Liberties Union filed a lawsuit challenging Executive Order 9066. The attorney bailed him out, but Mr. Korematsu was arrested and taken to Tanforan assembly internment camp. The case Korematsu v. United States Supreme Court claimed the detainment of loyal citizens was unconstitutional. It lost on 12/18/44 on the grounds that the compulsory exclusion was justified because of emergency and the military necessity to curtail the civil liberties of a specific racial group.

On 1/19/83, two attorneys brought Korematsu's case before the federal court in San Francisco, and the U.S. District Court formally vacated Korematsu's conviction. Korematsu said, "I would like to see the government admit that they were wrong and do something about it so this will never happen again to any American citizen of any race, creed, or color. If anyone should do any pardoning, I should be the one pardoning the government for what they did to the Japanese-American people."(1)

1/2/45: (Eight months before the end of the war) all internees were given $25 and a train ticket back to their former homes if they wanted to return.

Mine Okubo: 6/27/12-2/10/01: received her Master's of Fine Arts from UC Berkeley before she was interned at the Tanforan and Topaz internment camps. She had a realistic, creative, as well as humorous mind. Okubo documented life in an internment camp and wrote the book *Citizen 13660,* published in 1946 by the University of Washington Press. Cameras and photographs were not permitted in the camps, so she recorded everything in sketches, drawings, and paintings.

American Japanese Claims Act of 1948: To receive compensation for property losses, internees had to show proof. The IRS destroyed most of the 1939-42 tax records, and many were unable to establish their claims as valid.

Japanese Americans filed 26,568 claims totaling $148 million in requests; $37 million was approved and disbursed. Nothing was paid for internment time or for loss of earnings or profits.

Senate Bill 1009, 8/10/88: Restitution and apology. Payments of $20,000 went to each individual interned. A public education fund was sent up to help ensure that this would not happen again. Eighty-two thousand Japanese Americans received an apology and monetary redress.

Civil Liberties Act of 1988: Signed into law by President Reagan that the incarceration was a fundamental and grave injustice. "For these fundamental violations of the basic civil liberties and constitutional rights of these individuals of Japanese ancestry, the Congress apologizes on behalf of the Nation."

The fishing community on Terminal Island in San Pedro Bay, California, was evacuated and never re-established.

In 1952 Issei could become citizens.

Endnotes:
(1): Chin, Steven A., Ed. Alex Haley. *When Justice Failed: The Fred Korematsu Story*. Steck-Vaughn Co., New York, NY. 1993. Pg. 95.

References:
Alonso, Karen. *Korematsu v. United States*, Enslow Publishers, Springfield, N.J. 1998.

Burton, Jeffrey F.; Farrell, Mary M.; Lord, Florence B.; Lord, Richard W. *Confinement and Ethnicity: An Overview of World War II,* Chapter 3.

Chin, Steven A., Ed. Alex Haley. *When Justice Failed: The Fred Korematsu Story.* Steck-Vaughn Co., New York, NY. 1993.

Densho oral history website: "Densho: The Japanese-American Legacy Project," Director, Tom Ikeda. Free digital archive containing hundreds of video oral histories, photographs and documents. Http://www.densho.org.

Executive order 9066, (President Franklin D. Roosevelt, Doc. 42-1563; Filed, 2/21/42; 12:51 p.m.)

Hill, Kimi Kodai, ed. *Topaz Moon: Chiura Obata's Art of the Internment.* Berkeley: Heyday Books, 2000.

Inada, Lawson Fusao, ed. *Only What We Could Carry.* Berkeley: Heyday Books, 2000.

Japanese-American National Museum: Hirasaki National Resource Center, www.janm.org/nrc/accfact.php

Korematsu v. U.S., 1944WL 42849, Appellate Brief.

Okubo, Mine, *Citizen 13660,* Seattle: University of Washington Press, 1994.

Uchida, Yoshiko. *Desert Exile.* University of Washington Press, 1982.
www.bookmice.net/darkchilde/japan/camp2.html
www.janm.org/projects/clac/topaz.htm

http://academic.udayton.edu/race/02rights/intern04.
htm
http://www.tulelake.org/history.html
http://www.intimeandplace.org/Japanese%20interm
ent/reading/loyaltyquestions.html

History of Japanese-American Soldiers During WW II

- 20,000 Japanese-American men and women served in the U.S. Army during WW II.
- 3,000 Hawaiian and 800 Japanese-American men were inducted into the 442nd Infantry Regiment.
- The 442nd Regimental Combat Team was the most decorated unit, for its size and length of service, in the entire history of the U.S. Military. They suffered the highest casualty rate and were known as the "Purple Heart Battalion." More than 700 men were killed. The 4,000 men who initially came in April 1943 had to be replaced nearly 3.5 times. In total, about 14,000 men served, ultimately earning 9,486 Purple Hearts and an unprecedented eight Presidential Unit Citations. Twenty-one of its members were awarded Medals of Honor. Members of the 442nd received a total of 18,143 awards. The Japanese-American soldiers' average height was 5'3" and average weight 125 pounds.

References:

Asahina, Robert. *Just Americans: How Japanese-Americans Won a War at Home and Abroad.* Gotham Books, 2006.

Go For Broke! Madacy Music Group, Inc., Produced by
Dore Schary, 1951. Realistic movie about the Japanese-
American 442nd Regimental Combat Team.

Going For Broke, DVD documentary, distributed by Qestar,
Inc. Hosted by Senator Daniel K. Inouye.
http://www.sfmuseum.org/war/issei.html

Sadako Sasaki was two years old when the Hiroshima
bomb dropped near her home. By age 11 she was
diagnosed with leukemia, caused by radiation exposure
from the atomic bomb. Sadako folded paper cranes in the
hospital, according to the Japanese belief that if one folds
1,000 cranes they will be granted a wish. She was only
able to fold 644 cranes. Her wish was for world peace.
(Paper was very scarce at the time.) Sadako Sasaki died at
age 12, October 25, 1955. In 1958 a memorial was built for
her and all the children who had died from the effects of
the atomic bomb. It is a statue of Sadako Sasaki holding a
golden crane at the Hiroshima Peace Memorial, or
Genbaku Dome. At the foot of the statue is a plaque that
reads: "This is our cry. This is our prayer. Peace on
Earth." Today, over nine metric tons of paper cranes are
delivered to Hiroshima annually.

Corer, Eleanor. *Sadako and The Thousand Paper Cranes.*
Published by Puffin, 1977.
www.wikipedia.org/wiki/SadakoSasaki

History of the Tuskegee Airmen

Yancy Williams, a Howard University student, sued the government to become an aviation cadet. As a result, the Army Air Force, in November of 1941, set up a pilot training center for Negroes at Alabama's Tuskegee Institute (TAAF).

From 1941-1946, 994 pilots graduated from TAAF; 450 served overseas for combat duty.

Tuskegee Airmen shot down 251 enemy planes and logged more than 15,000 sorties. None of the bombers they escorted were ever shot down.

The 332nd Fighter Group lost 66 men and had 33 taken as prisoners. Among the 850 awards the group won were 150 Distinguished Flying Crosses, eight Purple Hearts, 14 Bronze Stars, and 744 Air Medals. The 332nd was the only fighter group in the entire Army that did not lose a bomber from enemy attack.

Freeman Field Mutiny, 4/11/45: 162 arrests of Black officers. Three were court-martialed, one convicted. **Lt. Roger Terry,** a Tuskegee airman, was court-martialed for jostling a White officer, was fined $150, reduced in rank, and dishonorably discharged in 11/45. He received a full pardon, restoration of rank, and a refund of his fine in 1995. The remaining officers received instructions for clearing their records.

The 477th was never deployed into combat.

Captain James Walker bailed out of his crippled fighter plane and landed in Belgrade. Seventeen-year-old **Aleksandr Zivkovic** found and hid him. Walker spent 39 days dodging Nazis with the help of the Serbs. Zivkovic immigrated to America in 1971 and reunited with Captain Walker. (1)

Benjamin O. Davis, Jr. became the first Black Army Air Force general.

Executive Order 9981, 1948: signed by President Harry S. Truman, racially integrated the United States Armed Services.

Endnotes:
(1) New York Daily News March 31, 1999.

References:
Brooks, Phillip. *The Tuskegee Airmen.* Compass Point Books, Minneapolis, Minn. 2005.

Homan, Lynn M. & Reilly, Thomas. *Black Knights: The Story of The Tuskegee Airmen.* Pelican Publishing Co., Gretna, LA. 2001.
http:www.tuskegeeairmen.org/Tuskegee_Airmen_Hitory.html

Warren, Lt. Col. James C. *The Tuskegee Airmen Mutiny at Freeman Field.* The Conyers Publishing Company. 2001.
http://en.wikipedia.org/wiki/Freeman_Field_Mutiny
http://www.tuskegeeairmen.org/uploads/Roger Terry. pdf

History of Working Women
During WW II

* Throughout WW II, more than 210,000 women were permanently disabled in factory accidents, and 37,000 died. (1)
* The average factory woman put in 48 hours over a six-day work week. (2)
* Women ages 14-50 worked in factories during WW II. (3)
* More women were working after WW II in 1947 than during the war; they were paid less for essential civilian work.
* Most women were laid off from better paying industrial jobs after the war. (4)

Endnotes:

(1) Ralph Lewis, Brenda. "War Labor Board equal pay for equal work," 1942. Reader's Digest: *Women At War*. New York. 2002. p. 79.

(2) Weatherford, Doris. *American Women and World War II*. New York: Facts on File, 1900. p. 162.

(3) Ralph Lewis, Brenda, pg. 79.

(4) Mersky, Leder. *Thanks for the Memories*. London: Praeger, 2006. p. 94-95.

History of Shipbuilding in Richmond, California, During WW II

There were four Richmond shipyards that built 747 ships during WW II, employing more than 90,000 people.

Liberty Ships were built in 13 states by 15 companies in 18 shipyards. A total of 2,751 Liberty Ships were built. A Liberty Ship cost under $2,000,000, was 441 feet long, and 56 feet wide. Her three-cylinder, reciprocating steam engine, fed by two oil-burning boilers, produced 2,000 hp and a speed of 11 knots. Its five holds could carry over 9,000 tons of cargo, plus airplanes, tanks, and locomotives lashed to its deck. It could carry 2,840 jeeps, 440 tanks, or 230 million rounds of rifle ammunition. A Liberty Ship could carry a crew of 44 and 12-25 Naval Armed Guards. It was slower and less strong than a Victory Ship. The *SS Robert E. Peary* Liberty Ship in Richmond held the record for being built in the shortest time, four days, 15 hours and 29 minutes after the keel was laid. This record has never been surpassed. She sailed on her maiden voyage 10 days later on November 22, 1942, carrying 43 seamen and 17 naval personnel. Liberty Ships were named after prominent deceased Americans. Eighteen were named for outstanding African Americans. Any group that raised $2 million in war bonds could suggest a name for a Liberty Ship. The founder of a 4-H group, the first Ukrainian immigrant to America, and an organizer for the International Ladies' Garment Union all had a Liberty Ship named after them. The *SS Jeremiah O'Brien* Liberty Ship was built in 1943, in So. Portland, Maine.

The ship is presently moored in San Francisco. Virtual walking tour: www.ssjeremiahobrien.org.

There were 531 **Victory Ships** built during WW II in six shipyards in the United States. They were larger and had greater horsepower engines than Liberty Ships. Victory Ships were 455 feet long, and had a speed of 15-17 knots. The *SS Red Oak* Victory Ship was built in Kaiser Richmond Shipyard #1, and was launched on 11/9/44. It is the only surviving vessel of the 747 that were built. To tour the ship go to ssredoakvictory.org.

There were 90,000 workers at the Richmond shipyards at their peak, diminishing to less than 35,000 by 8/45. In 1945, shipbuilding in the yards was shut down. The shipyards were dismantled by 7/45. Many ships were sold for scrap. There were approximately 10,000 people out of work.

Richmond's population: 23,642 in 1940, growing to 130,00 by April 1943. (1)

Endnotes:
(1) *The Second Gold Rush: Oakland and the East Bay in World War II.* Johnson, Marilynn S., University of California Press, 1996. pg. 33.

References:

Marinship. Finnie, Richard. Taylor & Taylor, San Francisco. 1947.

Rosie the Riveter web site:
www.rosietheriveter.org/shiphist.htm.

History of Child Care
in Richmond, California

Before the war, there were 7,000 children in Richmond. In September 1944 there were 35,000 children. (1)

At its peak, with 24,000 women on the Kaiser payroll, Richmond's citywide child facilities maintained a total daily attendance of 1,400 children. Thirty-five nursery schools were established in the Richmond area during WW II. (2)

The Lanham Act of 1941 provided federal funding for day care. It helped construct schools and other facilities in areas experiencing heavy migration due to the growth of defense industries. It did have many shortcomings. Funds were not made available until well into the war. Daycare during the war was never fully funded. (3)

Henry J. Kaiser (1882-1967) testified before Congress, arguing that services for women, including childcare facilities, were essential to improve the manpower situation and the government should finance them. (4) Kaiser directed the construction of Child Development Centers and sought advice from **Dr. Catherine Landreth (1899-1995)**, Doctor of Psychology, who wrote several books and articles about child development. Landreth was an innovative expert on enhancing child development in centers and how best they should be designed, interiorly as well as exteriorly. (5)

The Maritime Child Development Center was the first publicly funded center in the U.S. It was funded and constructed by the U.S. Maritime Commission. The center was heavily subsidized by Kaiser. (6) It had a total enrollment (not simultaneously) of 718 children in 1943-1944 with a capacity of 180 children per day. The center had a ratio of accredited teachers to children of one to six. (7)

A nurse, art instructor, music director, pediatrician, dental hygienist, psychiatrist, and librarian made the rounds of many centers in Richmond.

The centers did not serve many African-American children and Black women were not part of the administration or staff. (8)

In July 1944, 3,000 nursery schools were established in the United States. (9)

Endnotes:

(1) nps.gov/pwro/NatRegPullmanChildDevCenter.pdf.

(2) *Growing Pains*, Kaiser newsletter "For'N'Aft," September 1944, 8.

(3) Rose, Elizabeth. *A Mother's Job*, Oxford Press, 1999. Pg. 166 .

(4) Greenbaum, Lucy, "As Kaiser Sees It," *The New York Times*, 31 October 1943.

(5) Landreth, Catherine. *Education of the Young Child – A Nursery School Manuel*. John Wiley & Sons, Inc. NY 1942.

(6) Brown, Hubert Wen. *The Impact of War Worker Migration on the Public School System of Richmond California, from 1940 to 1945.*

(7) Ph.D. Diss., Stanford University, 1973, pg. 269.

(8) Johnson, Marilynn S. *The Second Gold Rush, To Place Our Deeds: The African-American Community in Richmond, CA.*

(9) Moore, Shirley Ann Wilson, *To Place Our Deeds*, University of California Press, Berkeley, CA, 2000. Pg. 68.

References:

nps.gov/pwro/NatRegPullmanChildDevCenter.pdf
nps.gov/pwro/NatRegMaritimeChildDevCenter.pdf

History of the Port Chicago Explosion

On July 17, 1944, 320 men (of whom 202 were African Americans) were instantly killed at the Port Chicago, California Naval base in Contra Costa County.

Port Chicago Mutiny 9/14/44: Fifty men refused to load munitions at Mare Island base after the Port Chicago explosion. The trial lasted six weeks. All 50 men were found guilty, sentenced to 15 years in prison and a dishonorable discharge. Forty-seven of the 50 were released in 1/46; three served additional months in prison. Two remained in the prison's hospital recuperating from injuries; one seaman was not released because of bad conduct.

On 1/46 the Navy granted clemency to the sailors from the Port Chicago base; 47 were paroled to active duty.

The Navy asked Congress to give each victim's family $5,000. Representative John E. Rankin of Mississippi had it reduced to $2,000 when he learned most of the victims were Black. (1) Congress settled on $3,000. "Of the 320 dead, only 51 could be identified." (2) The tombstones read "Unknown, US Navy, 17 July 1944." (3)

"In 1994, a review of the proceedings found that racism had played a role in the work at Port Chicago and in the subsequent mutiny proceedings." (4) In 1999, President Clinton officially pardoned **Fredrick Meeks,** one of the three surviving men who were tried in 1944, of any charges of mutiny." (5)

The Navy was desegregated in 6/45.

"The work done at Port Chicago was vital to the success of the war, yet the story of the men who carried out that work is often overlooked." (6)

The Port Chicago explosion accounted for 15 percent of all African-American deaths during WW II. (7)

Endnotes:

(1) Allen, Robert L. *The Port Chicago Mutiny*, Berkeley, CA. Heyday Books. 2006. P. 67. ISBN 9781597140287.

(2) http://www.history.navy.mil/faqs/faq80-4a.htm

(3) Bell, Christopher, and Elleman, Bruce, *Naval Mutinies of the Twentieth Century: An International Perspective.* Routledge. 2003.

(4) "Port Chicago—A Critical Link." National Park Service *Port Chicago Naval Magazine* National Memorial.

(5) Ibid.

(6) Ibid.

(7) Ibid.

To tour the Port Chicago, California Memorial site call 925-228-8860, web site: www.portchicagomemorial.org

Minority History During WW II

Over half a million African Americans left the South in the '40s to work for the war effort; 600,000 Black women were employed by the defense industry.

Forty-five thousand women, including 800 Native American women, served in the Armed Forces.

Twelve thousand Native American women left reservations for war jobs.

Half a million Mexican Americans enlisted in the Armed Forces.

Over 145,000 women were in war production jobs. In 10/45 there were only 37,000 employed. By 1946 over three million women left the workforce.

References:

Colman, Penny. *Rosie the Riveter. Women Working on the Home Front in World War II*. Crown Publishers, N.Y. 1995.

Giles, Nell. *Punch In, Susie! A Woman's War Factory Diary*. Harper & Brothers Pub., N.Y. 1943.

Gluck, Sherna Berger. *Rosie the Riveter Revisited*. Penguin Pub., N.Y. 1987.

Hinamatsuri Japanese Doll Festival: http://en.wikipedia.org/wiki/HinamatsuriKuriddm

Josephson, Judith Pinkerton. *Growing Up in World War II, 1941-1945*. Lerner Pub., Minneapolis. 2003.

Lewis, Edward V., O'Brien, and Robert O'Brien. *Ships*. Life Science Library. Time Inc., N.Y. 1965.

Litoff, Judy; Smith, David. *American Women in a World at War, Contemporary Accounts From World War II*. Scholarly Resources, Inc., Wilmington, Del. 1997.

Litoff, Judy; Smith, David. *Since You Went Away*. University of Kansas Press. 1991.

Moore, Christopher Paul. *Fighting For America, Black Soldiers-The Unsung Heroes of World War II*. Presidio Press, N.Y. 2006.

National Park Service, U.S. Department of the Interior. Rosie The Riveter/World War II Home Front National Historical Park.

Olian, Joanne. *Everyday Fashions of the Forties as Pictured in Sears Catalogs*. Dover Pub., N.Y. 1992.

Petersen, Christine. *Rosie the Riveter*. Scholastic Inc., N.Y. 2005.

Takaki, Ronald. *Double Victory, A Multicultural History of America in World War II*. Little, Brown & Co., N.Y. 2000.

Tateishi, John. *And Justice For All, An Oral History of the Japanese-American Detention Camps*. University of Washington Press, 1984.

Von Miklos, Josephine. *I Took a War Job*. Simon & Shuster, N.Y. 1943.

Wise, Nancy Baker, and Christy Wise. *A Mouthful of Rivets*. Kpsseu-Bass Inc., San Francisco, Ca. 1994.

Yellin, Emily. *Our Mothers' War, American Women at Home and at the Front During World War II*. Simon & Schuster, Inc., N.Y. 2004.

The American Girls Collection. *Welcome to Molly's World 1944, Growing up in World War Two America*. Pleasant Co. Publications, Middleton, WI. 1999.

Visit Richmond Museum of History, Richmond, CA: http://wwwrichmondmuseumofhistory.org

About the Author

starshotsphotography@gmail.com

Jeane Slone is the past vice president and a present board member of the California Redwood Writer's Club, a member of the Healdsburg Literary Guild, a member of the Military Writer's Society of America, and a member of the Pacific Coast Air Museum.

Jeane is the MC for the monthly event "Dine With Local Authors," and distributes local authors' books in local shops throughout Sonoma County. She is also a tutor for the Library Literacy Program.

Jeane received the prestigious Jack London Award for service to her club in 2015.

Ms. Slone has published the historical fictions: *She Flew Bombers*, winner of the national 2012 Indie Book Award (available as an audio book through audible.com);

She Built Ships During WW II (original and a version for ESL students); and *She Was an American Spy During WW II.*

All her novels are historically accurate, with characters who are a combination of fiction and real. The novels also contain over 25 historical photographs. These novels feature women who take men's roles during the war and experience gender and ethnic discrimination.

Please visit Jeane's web site for further information:

www.jeaneslone.com

JeaneSlone@eslpublishing.com

www.eslpublishing.com

About the ESL Editor

Michelle Deya Knoop has been teaching ESL since 1993 and coaching accent since 2010. She got her Master's Degree in TESOL at San Francisco State University in 1995 and teaches mostly in community colleges. Ms. Knoop has written numerous language teaching materials, including *A Brief History of Latin Rock Music in the U.S.A.* and *The American Accent Workbook*. She has lived in South Korea, Spain, Mexico, and Costa Rica. She speaks Spanish and a little Korean, as well as English. Knoop grew up in the heart of San Francisco and now lives in Sonoma County, California, with her family. She can be reached at accent@englishworks.us

Made in the USA
Columbia, SC
17 November 2024

46300480R00096